BIOLOGICAL WEAPONS
USING NATURE TO KILL

By Anna Collins

Portions of this book originally appeared in *Biological Warfare* by Don Nardo.

LUCENT
PRESS

Published in 2018 by
Lucent Press, an Imprint of Greenhaven Publishing, LLC
353 3rd Avenue
Suite 255
New York, NY 10010

Designer: Seth Hughes
Editor: Jennifer Lombardo

Library of Congress Cataloging-in-Publication Data

Names: Collins, Anna, author.
Title: Biological weapons : using nature to kill / by Anna Collins.
Description: New York : Lucent Press, [2018] | Series: Hot topics | Includes
    index.
Identifiers: LCCN 2017043214| ISBN 9781534562899 (pbk. book) | ISBN
    9781534562011 (library bound book)
Subjects: LCSH: Biological weapons. | Biological warfare. | Bioterrorism.
Classification: LCC UG447.8 .C655 2018 | DDC 358/.38–dc23
LC record available at https://lccn.loc.gov/2017043214

CPSIA compliance information: Batch #CW18KL: For further information contact Greenhaven Publishing LLC, New York,
New York at 1-844-317-7404.

Please visit our website, www.greenhavenpublishing.com. For a free color catalog of all our
high-quality books, call toll free 1-844-317-7404 or fax 1-844-317-7405.

CONTENTS

FOREWORD   4

INTRODUCTION   6
What Are Biological Weapons?

CHAPTER 1   10
The Effects of Biological Agents

CHAPTER 2   29
Biological Warfare in the 20th Century

CHAPTER 3   45
Bioterrorism: A Growing Concern

CHAPTER 4   59
Fighting Biological Attacks

CHAPTER 5   76
Preparing for the Future

NOTES   88

DISCUSSION QUESTIONS   93

ORGANIZATIONS TO CONTACT   95

FOR MORE INFORMATION   97

INDEX   99

PICTURE CREDITS   103

ABOUT THE AUTHOR   104

Adolescence is a time when many people begin to take notice of the world around them. News channels, blogs, and talk radio shows are constantly promoting one view or another; very few are unbiased. Young people also hear conflicting information from parents, friends, teachers, and acquaintances. Often, they will hear only one side of an issue or be given flawed information. People who are trying to support a particular viewpoint may cite inaccurate facts and statistics on their blogs, and news programs present many conflicting views of important issues in our society. In a world where it seems everyone has a platform to share their thoughts, it can be difficult to find unbiased, accurate information about important issues.

It is not only facts that are important. In blog posts, in comments on online videos, and on talk shows, people will share opinions that are not necessarily true or false, but can still have a strong impact. For example, many young people struggle with their body image. Seeing or hearing negative comments about particular body types online can have a huge effect on the way someone views himself or herself and may lead to depression and anxiety. Although it is important not to keep information hidden from young people under the guise of protecting them, it is equally important to offer encouragement on issues that affect their mental health.

The titles in the Hot Topics series provide readers with different viewpoints on important issues in today's society. Many of these issues, such as teen pregnancy and Internet safety, are of immediate concern to young people. This series aims to give readers factual context on these crucial topics in a way that lets them form their own opinions. The facts presented throughout also serve to empower readers to help themselves or support people they know who are struggling with many of the challenges adolescents face today. Although negative viewpoints are not ignored or downplayed, this series allows young people to see that the challenges they face are not insurmountable. Eating disorders can be overcome, the Internet can be navigated safely, and pregnant teens do not have to feel hopeless.

Quotes encompassing all viewpoints are presented and cited so readers can trace them back to their original source, verifying for themselves whether the information comes from a reputable place. Additional books and websites are listed, giving readers a starting point from which to continue their own research. Chapter questions encourage discussion, allowing young people to hear and understand their classmates' points of view as they further solidify their own. Full-color photographs and enlightening charts provide a deeper understanding of the topics at hand. All of these features augment the informative text, helping young people understand the world they live in and formulate their own opinions concerning the best way they can improve it.

What Are Biological Weapons?

The term biological warfare, also called germ warfare, refers to using deadly germs or poisons—biological weapons—to harm enemies. This may be done during a declared war or as a sneak attack on a group that is seen as an enemy. This is a practice that has been going on for centuries; according to *Encyclopedia Britannica*, "in many conflicts, diseases have been responsible for more deaths than all the employed combat arms combined, even when they have not consciously been used as weapons."[1]

One example of early biological warfare happened after English settlers began colonizing what is now the United States. Thousands—perhaps millions—of Native Americans were killed when they caught smallpox from the settlers. There is at least one written record of a British commander named Lord Jeffrey Amherst encouraging his troops to give the Native Americans blankets infected with the disease, knowing they did not have a resistance to it the way the white Europeans did. However, whether this plan was carried out in other parts of the country is unknown. Regardless, smallpox is highly contagious and would have spread quickly among Native American populations; whether they were infected on purpose or by accident does not change the fact that "[m]ore victims of colonization were killed by Eurasian germs, than by either the gun or the sword, making germs the deadliest agent of conquest."[2]

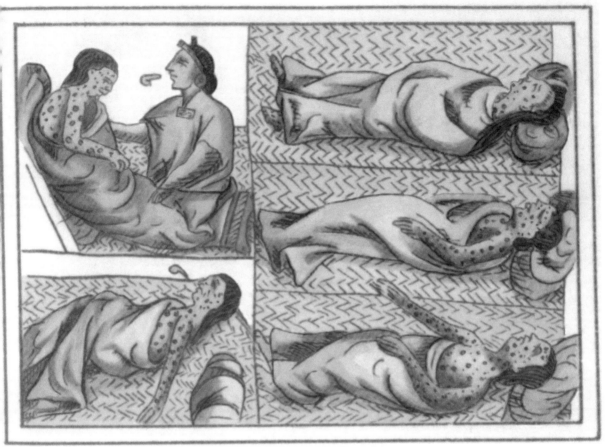

Huge portions of Native American populations were wiped out by smallpox when the Europeans came to North America.

Cheap and Easy

Today, biological weapons are cheaper and easier to make than other types of weapons, such as nuclear bombs. However, they tend to be less effective at killing large groups of people than other types of weapons. In the past, germs were helped by the conditions in which armies were fighting: They often endured long periods of coldness and dampness as well as a severe lack of food and sleep. Today, it is difficult for someone to infect many people at once with a germ or poison, but it is not impossible.

A number of countries, including the United States, the Soviet Union, Germany, Britain, and Japan, developed biological warfare programs in the 20th century. Though most countries have agreed to international treaties banning such weapons, experts warn that some nations may still maintain secret stockpiles. The Organization for the Prohibition of Chemical Weapons (OPCW) is working with nations to help or convince them to destroy these stockpiles.

What Is the Risk?

Having the ability to use biological weapons is one thing, and actually using them is quite another. The fact that so many countries thought of and agreed to international bans on such weapons shows that in general, organized societies do not have a strong intent to use them. Additionally, creating biological weapons involves using special substances and laboratory equipment. In the United States, these items are monitored by the government, and if someone buys them, they may be investigated. The threat of a biological attack is quite small; many experts say the average American should be more concerned about dying from heart disease than from a biological weapon.

However, it is not impossible for isolated individuals or groups, or even the government of a country, to decide to carry out a biological attack. A handful of horrifying events in recent years have brought home the reality that some terrorist groups and individuals are willing to do things that most people would consider immoral. These events include the destruction of a federal building in Oklahoma City in 1995 by Timothy McVeigh, an act that killed 168 people and injured more than 500; the attacks on September 11, 2001, in which members of al-Qaeda, headed by Osama bin Laden, killed around 3,000 people; the attacks carried out by Dylann Roof at a historically black church in Charleston, South Carolina, in 2015, in which 9 people died; and the 2016 shooting at Pulse Nightclub in Orlando, Florida, which was carried out by Omar Mateen and was the deadliest shooting in United States history.

In fact, terrorism expert Jim A. Davis has pointed out, some of these terrorists have claimed their attacks are moral according to their own personal religious and political beliefs. In this way, the concept of morality has been used both to ban and to justify the use of weapons of mass destruction. Although none of the attacks listed above used biological weapons, it is clear that some people may find ways to justify their use in the future if they want to do so. Since that small risk does remain, federal and state governments have departments dedicated to studying the various biological agents and creating action plans in case one of them is ever used in an attack.

CHAPTER 1

The Effects of Biological Agents

A biological agent is a disease or toxin (poison) that can potentially be used in biological warfare or bioterrorism. This may include bacteria, viruses, and fungi, among others. These are called microorganisms because they are so small they can only be seen with a microscope.

Many people are afraid of synthetic, or man-made, chemicals, but biological agents exist and have existed for a long time in varying amounts in nature. Generally, when a person encounters one of them in very small doses, it does little or no harm. It is only when large amounts of the agent are released in one place that the person becomes sick. This is true of just about any substance in nature. For instance, vitamin A is a necessary part of a healthy diet and plays an important role in building healthy bones and teeth. However, too much at once can cause blindness, bone deformities, and even death. Carrots, which are a good source of this nutrient, have about 167 international units (IU) of vitamin A per gram; in contrast, a polar bear's liver, which can kill a human if it is eaten, contains between 24,000 and 35,000 IU of vitamin A per gram.

However, even though vitamins and minerals can kill a person if they encounter too much at once, they are not considered biological weapons because they are not living organisms. Additionally, they are primarily helpful to humans; people are encouraged to seek them out, and it is rare for someone to die from an overdose. In contrast, biological agents are living things that are primarily dangerous to humans. Although they may be safe in tiny doses, it is incredibly easy for a person to die when they encounter large amounts of microorganisms such as anthrax and mold or are infected with a disease such as Ebola or smallpox. Some biological agents are fairly easy and inexpensive to weaponize, whereas others require a great deal of expertise and money to make them a real threat to human populations.

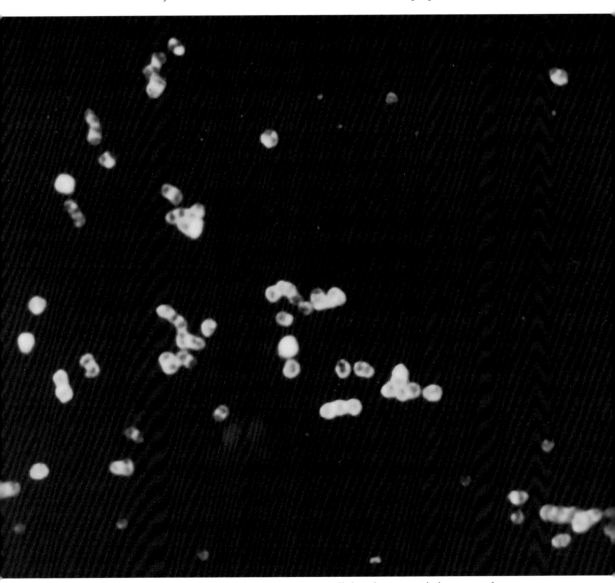

Microorganisms such as this bacteria are so small that they can only be seen under a microscope, but they can sometimes cause great harm to humans.

Choosing an Agent

A person or group planning a biological attack must take into account two major factors. First, the agent chosen must be harmful or deadly in large doses. Second, and just as important, the agent must be able to be weaponized using a reasonable amount of time, money, and effort. If it is not, turning the potential agent into an effective weapon is too difficult and expensive for the attacker.

There are at least 100 known biological agents. The Centers for Disease Control and Prevention (CDC) classifies them in three ways. Category A means they are easily disseminated (introduced into the environment) or spread from person to person, highly deadly, have the potential to cause public panic, and require special action to fight. Category B means they do not spread easily, are not very deadly, and only require health officials to observe the situation to make sure it does not get worse. Category C includes agents that could be a problem in the future because they are easily available, are easy to produce and disseminate, and have the potential to cause severe health problems.

In many cases, an agent can be weaponized by spraying it in the air as an aerosol. It can also be placed in food or water or distributed by an explosion. Some agents are easier to weaponize than others. Since there are so many agents, however, many have not been studied enough for researchers to say with certainty which ones are most easily weaponized or what their effects on a large group might be.

Anthrax is one of the most well-known biological agents. This is mainly because of the national scare that occurred shortly after the attacks on the World Trade Center and the Pentagon in September 2001, known as the September 11 attacks (often spoken of as 9/11). A number of reporters, politicians, and other people received small but deadly concentrations of anthrax spores in mailed envelopes, and five people died as a result. This was the first time a biological weapon had been used in the United States since it became a country, and this incident made officials realize they needed to start studying biological weapons so they would know how to respond to future attacks.

One way to weaponize some biological agents would be to aerosolize them so they can be sprayed into the air.

Although this was the first time anthrax captured national attention in the United States, as well as in other countries, the disease itself is far from new. For centuries, naturally produced anthrax has killed cattle, sheep, and other livestock, as well as occasionally a few humans. No one knew what caused the disease or how it spread until 1876, when German researcher Robert Koch discovered irrefutable evidence for what came to be known as the anthrax disease cycle. The cycle begins with the anthrax germs, which are a type of bacteria. After the

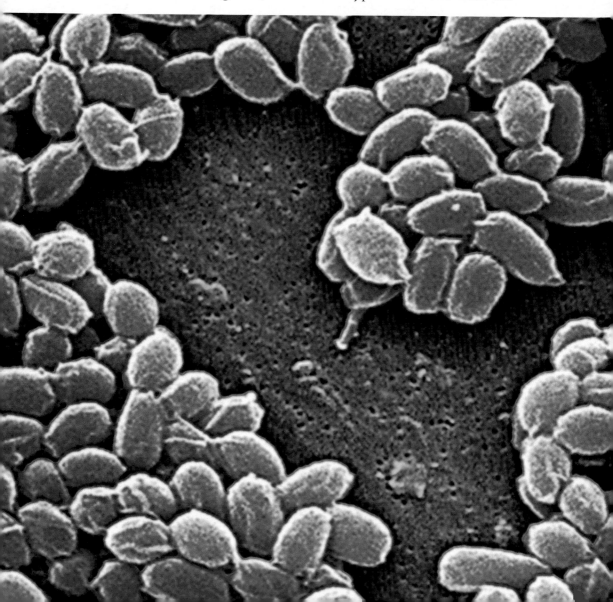

anthrax germs infect an animal, many of them change into spores, and some of these spores enter the soil. The spores are tough and resistant to extremes in temperature, so they can remain in the soil for months or even years, lying dormant until a healthy animal walks in the area and eats some grass or other plants in the infected area. In this way, the spores enter the animal's warm blood. There they spring to life, reproduce, infect the host, and finally revert to spore form, beginning the cycle once again.

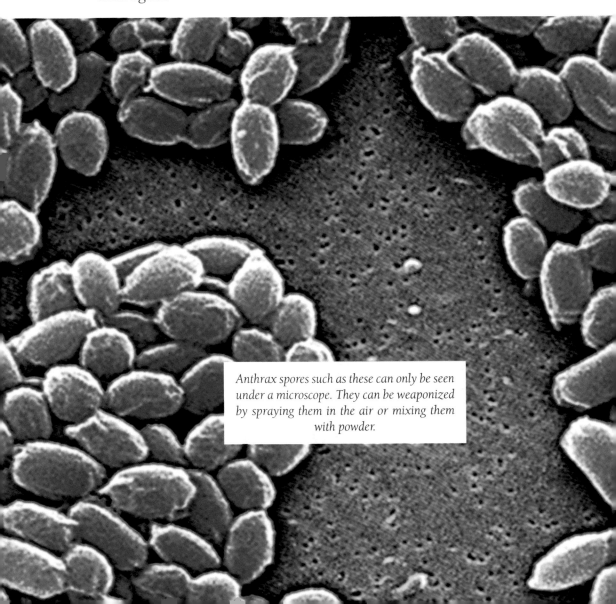

Anthrax spores such as these can only be seen under a microscope. They can be weaponized by spraying them in the air or mixing them with powder.

Anthrax spores can also pass from an infected animal to a human being, which makes it a Category A biological agent. Most naturally occurring human cases of anthrax have been among farmers and other people who come into regular, close contact with livestock. In the vast majority of these cases, the person catches the disease when spores enter the bloodstream through a cut, a form of transmission called cutaneous. Only a few people have contracted pulmonary anthrax, in which the spores directly enter the lungs. As biological warfare expert Eric Croddy explained,

> Of those who get infected with cutaneous anthrax … 10 to 20 percent are likely to die if the disease is left untreated. For pulmonary, or inhalation, anthrax, the rate is much higher. This form of the disease occurs when an individual breathes in thousands of spores and develops an infection that begins in the lungs. Left untreated, some 90 to 100 percent of people who contract inhalation anthrax may die.[3]

Symptoms of Cutaneous Anthrax

Jeanne Guillemin, an expert on biological agents, lists the symptoms of anthrax when it results from the spores making contact with a person's skin:

> In humans, an anthrax infection can begin in one of three ways. Infection through the skin (cutaneous anthrax) is … the most common and obvious form. It begins with a tiny pimple. In a few hours this eruption becomes a reddish-brown irritation and swelling that turns into an ulcer … that splits the skin. The black scablike crust that the lesion develops gives the disease its name, anthracis, the Latin transliteration of the Greek word for coal … Without treatment, the fatality rate for cutaneous anthrax can be 20 percent.[1]

1. Jeanne Guillemin, *Anthrax: The Investigation of a Deadly Outbreak.* Berkeley, CA: University of California Press, 1999, p. 4.

In the early years of the 20th century, people in some countries, notably Germany and Japan, saw the potential for using concentrated anthrax spores as a weapon. Later, the United States, the Soviet Union, and other nations also conducted experiments in weaponizing anthrax. Although people were afraid for a while that anthrax would become the weapon of choice for terrorists, that fear eventually decreased as time went on, and there were virtually no further attacks using biological weapons. The news website Reuters stated that as of 2017, "[m]ost scientific and security experts agree the risk remains relatively low."[4] Many countries have chosen to focus on chemical and nuclear weapons instead.

Fortunately, anthrax is generally not contagious from person to person. This means an attacker using weaponized anthrax spores can kill only as many people as they can directly expose to the spores. It is also fortunate that anthrax can be successfully treated with antibiotics in the early stages of an infection. The bad news, as Croddy wrote, is that infected people "may not know they are infected until they are well into the course of the infection. This is a very serious problem because anthrax needs to be treated quickly."[5]

ATTEMPTED MURDER OR JUST A SCARE?

"The letters accompanying the anthrax [mailed in 2001] … advised recipients to take antibiotics, implying that whoever had mailed them never really intended to harm anyone. But at least 17 people would fall ill and five would die."

–David Freed, journalist

David Freed, "The Wrong Man," *The Atlantic*, May 2010. www.theatlantic.com/magazine/archive/2010/05/the-wrong-man/308019/.

Botulism

Another substance that has killed people on a periodic basis throughout recorded history is a lethal poison known as the botulinum toxin, a Category A agent that causes botulism. Botulism is a serious condition acquired by eating spoiled food. The culprit behind the spoilage is a bacterium called *Clostridium botulinum*, which itself is not dangerous to animals or people. Instead, when these bacteria die and begin to decompose, they release the toxin, consisting of a tiny glob of protein, as a by-product.

What makes the botulinum toxin attractive to would-be biological attackers is its extreme lethality. It is among the most poisonous substances known; even a microscopic quantity is 100,000 times more dangerous than a dose of sarin nerve gas and can quickly kill a human. Within 24 hours of ingesting a sufficient amount of the toxin, a person would die of respiratory failure.

AN IMPORTANT CONSIDERATION

"Discussions of biological weapons usually address how hard it is to 'weaponize' the pathogens. For military use, weaponization is a requirement—agents must have predictable effects; they must be safe to store, easy to deploy, and subject to tight command control."

—John R. Moore, U.S. Navy Vietnam War veteran

John R. Moore, "North Korea's Stealth WMD," PJ Media, May 11, 2017. pjmedia.com/homeland-security/2017/05/11/north-koreas-stealth-wmd/.

Of course, poisoning a lot of food and then trying to get large numbers of people to eat it would obviously be very hard to do and would likely end up killing only a few people. Experts say the more efficient approach would be to find some way of getting the toxin into an aerosol spray or pouring it into a city's water supply. As Rutgers University scholar Leonard A. Cole pointed out,

> If a city's water purification system were blocked, a gallon of botulinum toxin in the water system could theoretically kill millions

[of people]. An innocent-looking fishing boat might encircle Man-hattan Island, blowing [the toxin] from an inconspicuous aerosol generator. Again, casualties could be in the millions. The boat and all traces of its activities would long be gone before the massive outbreak of [sickness] was apparent.[6]

Botulinum toxin is most commonly found in spoiled foods, especially canned foods. Home canning carries the biggest risk, but store-bought cans can also contain botulinum. Experts say a jar or can that is deeply dented or bulging should be thrown away unopened.

Weaponized Agents

Some biological agents, such as botulinum toxin, are relatively easy to produce. A small makeshift lab in someone's garage or basement could potentially create large quantities of these substances over time. The same is true of the Category B biological agent Q fever. Scientists gave it this name, in which the Q stands for query, because at first, they had difficulty understanding it and how it works. Q fever is caused by a bacterium called *Coxiella burnetii*, which can be transmitted by ticks as well as the urine of cattle, sheep, and goats.

Q fever can easily be created in larger amounts by culturing the microbes in chicken eggs. Many billions of *C. burnetii* could be produced in a single egg. The germs could then be weaponized like many other biological agents.

Two other Category B biological agents that could be produced in a fairly small and unsophisticated lab are ricin and saxitoxin. Both consist of proteins that are highly poisonous to humans. Ricin can be extracted from the castor plant using relatively simple laboratory procedures. Experts say ricin is difficult to weaponize but point out that an individual or group with sufficient time, money, and resources could do it. "Ricin is considered a real threat," Croddy wrote, "and research continues in the United States to develop treatment and [a] vaccine for it."[7]

Saxitoxin could be even more deadly than ricin if effectively weaponized and unleashed by attackers. Saxitoxin comes from microscopic algae found in the oceans. When enough of these germs come together in one area, they form what is called a red tide, which infects local shellfish; when someone eats the shellfish, he or she can die in two to twelve hours if the illness is not recognized and treated. The toxin can also be grown in a lab. Someone could place a large concentration of the toxin in a bomb and explode it in a crowded area. Some of the toxin would then become airborne, and people would breathe it in. Since this has not yet happened, experts are unsure of what would happen if someone breathed it in, but experiments done with animals suggest a person would die within minutes.

R_0

Scientists use a number called the R_0 (pronounced "r-naught") to describe how contagious a disease is and how many times the infection will reproduce itself as it spreads. According to Healthline,

> R_0 tells you the average number of people who will catch a disease from one contagious person. It specifically applies to a population of people who were previously free of infection and haven't been vaccinated. If a disease has an R_0 of 18, a person who has the disease will transmit it to an average of 18 other people, as long as no one has been vaccinated against it or is already immune to it in their community ...
>
> Importantly, a disease's R_0 value only applies when everyone in a population is completely vulnerable to the disease. This means:
>
> • no one has been vaccinated
>
> • no one has had the disease before
>
> • there's no way to control the spread of the disease[1]

Measles has one of the highest R_0 values at 12 to 18. Ebola has one of the lowest at 2. Smallpox is in the middle with an R_0 of about 6. Health officials worry about smallpox in particular being used as a biological weapon because almost no one has been vaccinated since the disease was eradicated in 1972. A vaccine does exist, but it would be useless after someone has already caught the disease, so it is unclear how effective it would be in controlling its spread.

1. "What Is R_0? Gauging Contagious Infections," Healthline, accessed August 22, 2017. www.healthline.com/health/r-nought-reproduction-number#overview1.

Smallpox and Other Biological Agents

Some biological agents are potentially deadly but difficult or expensive for terrorists to get ahold of or weaponize. One of these is smallpox, which is a Category A agent. Among the characteristic symptoms of smallpox are high fever, chills, pain, eruptions of pus-filled sores, and, in about a third of all cases, death. Unlike anthrax, smallpox is caused by a virus rather than a bacterium, is mainly a disease of humans rather than animals, and is highly contagious. The disease "spreads person to person," medical expert Brenda J. McEleney wrote,

> via inhalation of [tiny] water droplets … exhaled by infected individuals. However, as with common-cold viruses, the smallpox virus can be introduced into the human body by touching a contaminated object, then subsequently touching one's nose or mouth with the contaminated hand.[8]

For thousands of years, the disease has spread through towns and countries around the world, leaving a trail of misery and death. So many people died when the disease struck ancient Rome, for instance, that there were not enough wagons to carry the dead out of the city. Over the centuries, other outbreaks of smallpox wiped out hundreds of thousands of people in China, Europe, and Central America.

Thanks to a vaccine developed by an 18th-century doctor named Edward Jenner, the death toll from smallpox began to decrease dramatically in the 1800s. Over time, the governments of most industrialized countries initiated programs to vaccinate most of their inhabitants. However, in less-developed nations, poverty and inadequate medical facilities frequently prevented large-scale vaccination programs. Thus, even as late as 1967, 10 million cases of the disease were reported worldwide.

Disturbed by these figures, in the late 1960s, the World Health Organization (WHO) decided to try to eradicate smallpox once and for all. The agency sent out hundreds of teams of doctors to vaccinate people whenever and wherever outbreaks of the illness were reported. Thanks to this effort, success came with astounding swiftness. In October 1977, the last known case of the disease was reported in Africa, and WHO proudly declared that smallpox had been eliminated.

Elimination of a disease means people today do not carry it and cannot pass it to others. However, some samples of the virus remain. They are kept for research purposes in two labs—one in the United States, the other in Siberia, Russia. These locations are very secure, so a terrorist group or individual would have to come up with a complicated plan to break in and steal the samples before they could ever use them. Additionally, experts have said the terrorists would need their own high-tech lab and expert knowledge of viruses, which most of them do not have. If smallpox were weaponized, it would be devastating, but the chances of that happening are currently slim. Other such biological agents include typhus (Category B), yellow fever (Category C), and bovine spongiform encephalopathy, or "mad cow" disease (Category C).

Hysteria and Infection

One concern among experts is whether a biological agent is contagious. A biological attack may directly affect only a few people, but if the agent used is something that can quickly be spread through the air, it will soon affect many more. This is why medical experts recommend vaccination. If the majority of a population is vaccinated, it creates herd immunity, which is "when a high percentage of the population is protected through vaccination against a virus or bacteria, making it difficult for a disease to spread because there are so few susceptible people left to infect."[9] The only people who should not be vaccinated are those who are medically unable to be, such as babies, people who have problems with their immune system, and people who are too sick with another disease, such as cancer. If too many people choose not to be vaccinated, though, herd immunity stops working, and these people as well as healthy people will become ill as the disease spreads from person to person. Health experts say herd immunity is an important part of reducing the danger of a biological attack.

Although some biological agents, such as smallpox and the bubonic plague, are incredibly contagious and deadly, many are not. For example, although Q fever is contagious, it would do little more than make people sick for a few days. Ricin, which can cause death within 36 to 72 hours, is not spread from person to person; someone must come into direct contact with it, either by eating castor beans or inhaling ricin powder. However, these agents could still cause widespread fear and panic in a given city or society, which many experts say is the true danger. In fact, mass hysteria—uncontrolled panic in a large group of people—is a danger during any high-risk situation. When people are hysterical, they do not think clearly, and this can lead to dangerous situations. For instance, in 2003, a security guard at Chicago's E2 nightclub used pepper spray to break up a fight. The club was severely overcrowded; it was made to hold 240 people, but there were more than 1,100 people there that night. As partiers tried to run from the pepper spray, they lost sight of everything except getting themselves out of the building. When people tripped and fell, they were trampled. In all, 21 people died as a result of the stampede.

Panic is one dangerous outcome of a biological attack. When people in a crowd such as this one do not remain calm, it is easy for some of them to get hurt or killed.

Should the Media Report Terrorist Attacks?

At a 2001 seminar given by the Royal College of Physicians in England, "speakers suggested that biological weapons were 'not very good' at causing death or destruction, but they warned of the dangers of public panic and loss of confidence in the authorities."[10] The media often plays a large role in increasing public hysteria—so much so that some people have suggested it is better for them not to report anything at all. Others disagree, saying the public deserves to be informed, but in a responsible way that minimizes panic. News outlets often report potential negative effects without letting viewers know that the risk of such effects is very small, causing people to become more worried than necessary. For example, in 2014, eight people in the United States were diagnosed with Ebola, a disease that is deadly if left untreated and that has severe effects, such as dehydration and coughing up blood. Fear of an epidemic swept the nation despite the fact that Ebola is only contagious if a person comes into direct contact with an infected patient's blood or other bodily fluids; it cannot be spread through the air by sneezing or coughing. Many news outlets did not talk about this low risk of catching the disease. According to news anchor Shepard Smith, the coverage of Ebola was irresponsible because it increased mass hysteria. He explained a key part of the news coverage:

> You have to remember that in the middle of all of this ... there is politics in the mix. With midterm elections coming, the party in charge needs to appear to be effectively leading. The party out of power needs to show that there is a lack of leadership. So the president has canceled a fundraising trip and is holding meetings and his political opponents are accusing his administration of poor leadership.[11]

Mass hysteria surrounding a biological attack would have many potential negative effects. These include:

- causing people to lose trust in government or health officials; if people were suspicious that they were not being told the whole truth, they might not listen to the important health information officials try to give

Shepard Smith, shown here, was one reporter who criticized sensationalized information during the Ebola outbreak.

- causing people to act dangerously out of fear; for instance, by intentionally or unintentionally harming others

- putting a strain on the health care system as people convince themselves they are victims of whichever biological agent was used in the attack and seek un-needed medical help

There may be other negative effects, but experts are unsure exactly what those might be, since the United States has not yet seen an effective large-scale biological attack. Some believe that if the media does not engage in scare tactics, there may not be any panic at all. However, according to Simon Wessely, a professor of psychological medicine, society has already seen a phenomenon called mass sociogenic (also called psychogenic) illness, in which people imagine they are having a reaction to a biological attack. He explained,

> *On September [29] 2001 paint fumes set off a bioterrorism scare at a middle school in Washington state, sending 16 students and a teacher to the hospital. On October [3] over 1000 students in several schools in Manila, Philippines, deluged local clinics with mundane flu-like symptoms such as cough, cold, and mild fever after rumours spread via short text services that the symptoms were due to bioterrorism. On October [9] a man sprayed an unknown substance into a Maryland subway station, resulting in the sudden appearance of nausea, headache, and sore throat in 35 people. It was later determined that the bottle contained window cleaner.*[12]

The rise of social media in recent years has increased the risk of rumors and false information being spread quickly. *Psychology Today* described one such case in 2011, in which 18 teenage girls from Le Roy, New York, and 1 nurse suddenly developed an unknown illness that caused muscle spasms and twitches, seemingly for no reason. After many tests, it was deter-mined that although the girls were not faking their symptoms, they did not have a real illness; the cause was psychological. Psychologist Romeo Vitelli noted that the nurse who displayed symptoms did not know the girls; she developed the same mystery illness after reading about them on Facebook. Additionally, for most of the teenage girls, "their symptoms only began after seeing a YouTube video posted by Lori Brownell, a girl with severe tics [muscle twitches] living in a neighbouring city."[13] In the case of a biological attack, false information could easily be spread through social media, leading to some of the negative effects described above. It is important for people to do research on a topic, look at multiple reputable news sources, and get their information from experts rather than social media posts.

CHAPTER 2

Biological Warfare in the 20th Century

Some countries have developed biological weapons as a way to defend themselves against potential attacks. At the time of development, many governments kept these projects secret. However, as of 2017, it is known that 16 countries as well as Taiwan—whose status as a country is disputed by China—have had or are currently suspected of having developed biological weapons: Canada, France, China, Cuba, Iran, Iraq, Germany, Israel, Japan, Russia, Libya, Syria, North Korea, South Africa, the United Kingdom, and the United States.

State-sponsored biological warfare projects were condemned and largely banned by international conventions in the 20th century. However, many experts believe such programs still exist in some countries. For example, in 2016, Russia accused the United States of building laboratories in Europe, but the United States denied these claims. Any country that does have biological weapons is not likely to announce that fact.

Many governments created biological weapons in the past, and some experts worry that these countries have not gotten rid of all their weapons and notes on how to make them. They fear the temptation to use them will prove too much for some countries to resist.

Unit 731

Although many nations have studied and experimented with biological weapons in recent times, most of these programs have been secret, and their details rarely come to light. One exception is Japan's biological warfare program, the details of which emerged after that nation's defeat in World War II. Allied investigators discovered that Japanese leaders had launched what they called Unit 731 in a facility located in a remote area of Manchuria, which the Japanese had taken from the Chinese. About 3,000 scientists and technicians worked at the complex, which studied anthrax, cholera, bubonic plague, typhus, tetanus, smallpox, botulinum toxin, tick encephalitis, and tuberculosis. The researchers conducted tests on human subjects, mostly prisoners of war, including Chinese, Koreans, and Mongolians. The prisoners were injected with or fed biological agents to see how humans would react to them. The researchers also experimented with different ways to weaponize biological agents. This included putting anthrax in chocolate, gum, fountain pens, umbrellas, and hot air balloons; creating bombs that would spread the plague; and putting cholera and typhoid into their enemies' water supplies. The prisoners who survived were set free at the end of the war and warned not to speak about what had happened in the facility, but eventually, the truth was discovered.

The remains of Unit 731 can still be seen today.

Government Bioweapons Programs

These current worries about ongoing state-sponsored biological warfare efforts are based on the realities of the bioweapons programs that came into being in the 20th century. In the early 1900s, as the new science of microbiology progressed rapidly, a number of scientists and government officials in various countries recognized the potential of germs as weapons. As time went on, state-sponsored research into biological weapons was kept secret because no country wanted to be accused of conducting research into weapons widely viewed as inhumane.

However, this research did continue, at first mainly in richer industrialized countries that could afford to fund the scientists and expensive labs required. Germany was an early leader in this work. During World War I, United States and British officials accused the Germans of developing biological weapons. Proof later emerged that the Germans had infected horses and cattle with anthrax in 1916 and 1917, hoping these animals would spread the disease to their enemies in Bucharest and France.

Though the Russians (at this time called Soviets) condemned the German biological warfare programs, they were soon engaged in similar programs that eventually far outstripped anything Germany had produced. The Soviet experiments in the following decades were dangerous in two ways, the most obvious being that the weapons produced posed a threat to other nations. The Soviet bioweapons programs also showed clearly that unanticipated accidents can occur during such research. In 1941, for example, the Soviets conducted biological experiments on political prisoners in Mongolia. Some of the victims were placed in cells with rats infested with fleas carrying bubonic plague germs. The prisoners contracted the disease. Then, some of them, still infested with fleas, escaped and infected the residents of some nearby Mongolian villages. Within a few weeks, 3,000 to 5,000 people died of the plague.

Another Soviet bioweapons accident took place in 1979. A secret biological warfare facility in the town of Sverdlovsk accidentally released deadly anthrax spores that had been weaponized in an aerosol spray. The spray traveled downwind to the town and infected 94 people. Sixty-six of them died within six weeks, which made it the deadliest anthrax infection in history.

HOW SOCIAL MEDIA HELPS TERRORISTS

"[Terrorists] use social networks to recruit, to inspire, and to connect, but they also rely on social media bystanders—everyday, regular people—to spread the impacts of their terror further than they could themselves, and to confuse authorities with misinformation ... stop and think before you hit Like or Retweet or Share."

—Emily Dreyfuss, journalist

Emily Dreyfuss, "Think Before You Tweet in the Wake of an Attack," *Wired*, May 23, 2017. www.wired.com/2017/05/think-tweet-wake-attack/.

In the meantime, the Americans, who had long condemned the German and Soviet bioweapons programs, were secretly developing their own. In the 1940s, the U.S. government spent more than $40 million on biological weapons research. A large portion of this money went into building a weapons plant in Vigo, Indiana, which, when fully operational, had the capability of producing up to 1.5 million biological bombs per month. After World War II, the Vigo plant was converted to produce medicines, but U.S. biological weapons research continued. Documents that were declassified in 2002 showed that the U.S. government tested chemical and biological weapons in America in the 1960s and 1970s—something many people would have protested if they had known about it. These tests, known as Project 112, were carried out mainly in Hawaii, Maryland, and Florida; for instance, a bacterium called *Bacillus globigii* was sprayed over Hawaii in 1965 so experts could make a plan to combat a real attack. The bacterium was thought to be harmless, but researchers later found out it could infect people whose immune systems were already weakened. Project 112 was not the first such experiment to be carried out, though; in 1950, the U.S. Navy spent a week spraying two kinds of bacteria into the air over San Francisco, California, to see how the city would be affected by a biological attack. No one in the city was informed. It is unknown how many people were infected, but it is known that at least one person died.

Hawaii was one place where the U.S. government secretly sprayed bacteria to simulate a real biological attack.

In another test, performed in 1966, a biological agent called *Bacillus subtilis*, which is similar to anthrax but harmless to humans, was secretly put into light bulbs in New York City's subway system to see how quickly a biological agent could spread in that environment. When the researchers broke the light bulbs, the spores were released. Many people noticed them but assumed they were normal dust or dirt; no one reported anything suspicious. The test's results showed that because the trains would push the contaminated air through the tunnels, up to 1 million people could be exposed.

The British also developed their own biological weapons program that experimented with anthrax and a number of other biological agents. As is true of the Soviet and American programs, the knowledge accumulated by the British in this area still exists in classified documents, and these documents remain a potential threat to the world because of the possibility that they might fall into the wrong hands.

The British, like the Soviets, demonstrated that the other major potential bioweapons threat—namely the possibility of accidents or unintended results—is very real. In 1942, for example, British researchers exploded a bomb laden with anthrax spores near a herd of sheep on the Scottish island of Gruinard. Afterward, they buried the sheep, but one of the infected corpses fell into the sea and floated to the coast of mainland Scotland, where about 30 local animals contracted anthrax. It is unsure whether any humans were infected, but fortunately, no one died and the disease was quickly contained. The island was disinfected, but even today, many people in the region still call Gruinard "Anthrax Island." After the anthrax-laced letters were mailed in 2001, many journalists visited the island in biohazard suits, hoping to learn whether the island could be a potential danger by providing terrorists with a source of anthrax. However, most locals who visit the island to hunt deer have said they have never gotten sick there.

Biological versus Chemical Weapons

Many people confuse biological and chemical weapons, but they are quite different. According to *The Guardian*, "Chemical weapons—often referred to as gases—suffocate the victim or cause massive burning. Biological weapons are slower acting, spreading a disease such as anthrax or smallpox through a population before the first signs are noticed."[1] Chemical weapons are made in a lab like biological weapons, but instead of using living substances, such as germs or toxic plant material, they use chemicals. Some deadly chemical weapons include mustard gas, sarin gas, and chlorine gas.

1. Simon Jeffery and Joe Plomin, "Biological and Chemical Weapons," *The Guardian*, October 31, 2001. www.theguardian.com/world/2001/oct/31/qanda.september11.

Anti-Bioweapon Conventions

Experts in biological warfare point out that many people are under the impression that such accidents are no longer possible because state-sponsored bioweapons programs have been banned by international law. However, this assumption is only partly true. On one hand, international conventions against the development of biological warfare programs were put in place in the 20th century. On the other, not all nations adopted these conventions. Moreover, some experts believe even some of those who did express support for the conventions have continued to conduct experiments in secret, thereby violating the conventions.

These anti–biological warfare conventions have both strengths and weaknesses as international safeguards. The first major convention of this type was the so-called Geneva Protocol, enacted in 1925. The full name of the treaty was the Protocol for the Prohibition of the Use in War of Asphyxiating, Poisonous or Other Gases and of Bacteriological Methods of Warfare. The term "bacteriological methods" was the then-current term for what are now called "biological weapons." Several nations immediately signed the Geneva Protocol. However, a number of others did not—among them the United States. The reason was that U.S. leaders did not want to risk worldwide condemnation if and when they felt they needed to use such weapons against enemies of the United States. It was not until 1975 that the United States finally ratified the protocol.

In the long run, the Geneva Protocol failed to stop the spread of biological agents and weapons, partly because its wording was vague and its bans limited. The document prohibited only the *use* of such bioweapons, for instance. The protocol did not forbid continued research and development, nor did it provide for international inspections of facilities suspected of breaking the treaty.

By the 1960s and 1970s, scientists, political leaders, and concerned public groups around the world saw the need for a new international convention that would supplement and strengthen the Geneva Protocol. In addition, a few national leaders were,

Most countries in the United Nations have signed or ratified the Biological Warfare Convention.

for the first time, willing to call for the elimination of their own biological programs and stockpiles. In 1969, for example, President Richard Nixon ordered that all U.S. biological weapons be destroyed. This dramatic and unprecedented move had the effect of setting the proper standard for the creation of the new international protocol. On April 10, 1972, the United States, the Soviet Union, and 85 other countries signed the Biological Warfare Convention (BWC). This agreement, which was ratified by the United Nations, bans the use of biological weapons. It states explicitly,

> Each State Party to this Convention undertakes never in any circumstances to develop, produce, stockpile or otherwise acquire or retain:
>
> (1) Microbial or other biological agents, or toxins whatever their origin or method of production, of types and in quantities that have no justification for … protective or other peaceful purposes;
>
> (2) Weapons, equipment or means of delivery designed to use such agents or toxins for hostile purposes or in armed conflict.[14]

This part of the BWC prohibits only the making of biological weapons. Another section of the agreement addresses the problem of eradicating existing stockpiles of weapons:

> Each State Party to this Convention undertakes to destroy, or to divert to peaceful purposes, as soon as possible … all agents, toxins, weapons, equipment and means of delivery … which are in its possession or under its jurisdiction or control. In implementing the provisions of this article all necessary safety precautions shall be observed to protect populations and the environment.[15]

As of 2017, 178 countries have ratified the BWC, which means they have agreed to abide by its rules. Six countries have signed it but not ratified it, which means they are considering abiding by the rules but have not decided yet. Twelve countries have done neither.

The Cold War

The natural question is whether or not the countries that ratified the BWC have complied with these provisions. The answer in at least some cases is no. The United States and other nations suspected that the Soviet Union was continuing its bioweapons programs in violation of the BWC. This was proven true when it was discovered that after signing the BWC, the Soviets had kept in operation 52 research facilities, weapons production plants, cover operations, and other workshops employing a total of more than 65,000 people. The accident involving the release of anthrax spores at Sverdlovsk in 1979 also showed that the Soviet Union had kept its weaponized anthrax stockpiles in violation of the treaty.

During the Cold War, the Soviet Union, whose flag is shown here, experimented with biological weapons because it believed the United States was doing the same.

International journalists later discovered and revealed that the Soviets broke their word largely due to lack of trust. Soviet leaders simply did not believe that the Americans had actually destroyed their own biological stockpiles in the 1960s and 1970s, which was in the middle of what was known as the Cold War—a period of tension between the United States and the Soviet Union. Croddy explained,

> The thinking inside the Soviet Union ... was that with the United States continuing its offensive research [into biological weapons], the USSR [Soviet Union] had no choice but to continue as well. And proceed they did: The microbes considered most suitable for weaponization included smallpox virus, anthrax, and plague bacteria, but the Soviet military planners and scientists also studied some 50 other biological agents. Most startling ... [was] the immense scale of the smallpox program, and the fact that tons of smallpox agent were weaponized for delivery in intercontinental ballistic missiles.[16]

There was a definite change of policy, however, following the collapse of the Soviet Union in the early 1990s. In 1992, the leaders of the now-sovereign state of Russia decided it was time to comply with the provisions of the BWC, and they shut down some of the offending biological weapons facilities. However, others remain operational today. Because these facilities are off-limits to outsiders, it is unclear whether they are in compliance with the treaty. The Russians claim that the buildings are used only to store old supplies of germ cultures, not to make new ones. However, as a number of experts point out, the very fact that these supplies have not been destroyed is itself a violation of the BWC.

Some Western observers are also suspicious that an undetermined amount of research into the development of new bioweapons may still be taking place in secret Russian labs. These fears seemed to have been strengthened by a revelation that came to light in 1997, when Russian scientists admitted to creating a strain of vaccine-resistant anthrax.

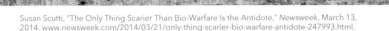

ACCIDENTS CAN BE DEADLY

"[In 1985], then Russian president Boris Yeltsin finally admitted that a military research facility ... had accidentally released spores of 'Anthrax 836' into the air [in 1972] ... the leak occurred because workers forgot to replace a filter in the facility's exhaust system ... had the wind been blowing in a different direction the day of the leak, hundreds of thousands could have died."

—Susan Scutti, journalist

Susan Scutti, "The Only Thing Scarier Than Bio-Warfare Is the Antidote," *Newsweek*, March 13, 2014. www.newsweek.com/2014/03/21/only-thing-scarier-bio-warfare-antidote-247993.html.

The Fear of Rogue States and Terrorists

The Russian scientists in question later cooperated with Western scientists and revealed how they made their new anthrax agent. However, both biological warfare experts and public officials in many countries are worried about other rogue states, which are countries that break international law in a way that poses a threat to nearby countries or the rest of the world. One rogue state that the international community worried about in this regard was Iraq, which was ruled by dictator Saddam Hussein until 2003. It had long been suspected that Iraq had been doing research into biological warfare. That nation signed the BWC in 1972, but Hussein's government officially ratified the treaty only when it was forced to do so after Iraq's defeat in the Gulf War of 1991. Following that conflict, United Nations weapons inspectors entered Iraq and revealed at least some of the extent of the Iraqi bioweapons program. In large part, the program operated under the direction of Dr. Rihab Rashid Taha. Captured during the U.S. invasion of Iraq in 2003, Taha admitted to making around 5,000 gallons (19,000 L) of botulinum toxin; 2,100 gallons (8,000 L) of anthrax spores; 530 gallons (2,000 L) of cancer-causing toxins; and considerable quantities of camel pox, a disease similar in many ways to smallpox. According to Taha and some other former Iraqi scientists and

North Korea is considered a rogue state because it often does not follow international law.

officials, most or all of these stockpiles were destroyed before 2003. This may be true, since in the wake of the U.S. invasion, inspectors were unable find them. Taha was later released by the Americans in exchange for her cooperation.

Although Iraq is, at least at present, no longer a biological threat to the world community, another rogue state, North Korea, greatly worries many American and other Western observers. According to the Arms Control Association, an organization founded in 1971 to promote understanding and support for policies to control various kinds of weapons:

> The 2010 State Department report on compliance with the BWC remarks that North Korea may "still consider the use of biological weapons as a military option." In a 2012 Ministry of National Defense White Paper, South Korea asserted that "North Korea likely has the capability to produce [...] anthrax, smallpox, pest, francisella tularensis, and hemorrhagic fever viruses."[17]

Because North Korea is a closed society with a secretive government, little is known for sure about its biological weapons program, so it is unknown whether these claims are true. However, officials take accusations such as these seriously and continue to monitor North Korea for signs that it may launch a biological attack, even though it has ratified the BWC.

Other rogue states suspected of having biowarfare programs are Syria and Taiwan. In April 2017, the Syrian government was accused of using chemical weapons on its citizens during the country's ongoing civil war—a claim the government denied. In 2013, Syria admitted to having a stockpile of chemical weapons, which were then destroyed. If it did attack rebel fighters in 2017, this would mean Syrian president Bashar al-Assad had lied about destroying all the chemical weapons. This has made experts question whether the country also secretly has stockpiles of biological weapons.

In addition to the threats posed by rogue states with biological weapons programs, many people fear that terrorist groups or individuals might develop their own biological weapons without the permission of their country's government. Biowarfare expert Tara O'Toole warned that private extremist and terrorist groups that are not officially connected to an established nation are much less likely to be discouraged by fears of revenge from the country they are attacking. Groups such as the Islamic State of Iraq and Syria (ISIS) have already used chemical weapons in Iraq and Syria, so experts do not believe they would hesitate to use biological weapons if they could. In 2015, the European Parliament was warned by experts that "the radical Islamic group has money; scientists—some of foreign origin—on the payroll; found an abundance of deadly toxins stockpiled by the tyrants of Syria, Iraq and Libya; and could make more of its own quite easily."[18] Thus, the first large-scale biological attack of the 21st century, if it does occur, may well be carried out by terrorists, and experts warn that governments should be prepared for that possibility.

CHAPTER 3

Bioterrorism: A Growing Concern

The threat of terrorism is not new; it has been going on all around the world for thousands of years. A terrorist is a person who tries to cause fear, often through violence and generally to achieve a political goal. In cases of war or revolution, these groups may call themselves rebels, while their opponents may call them terrorists. Early groups that could be considered to be terrorists include the Sons of Liberty, who led uprisings that sometimes turned violent against the British in the years leading up to the American Revolution; the Jacobins, who took power after the French Revolution and beheaded many French nobles; and the Fenian Brotherhood, an Irish group created in 1858 to rise up against the British, who controlled Ireland at that time.

In recent decades, many people have come to associate terrorism with radical Muslims—so much so that when other groups perform similar actions, news outlets often do not call them terrorists. For instance, in May 2017, a white supremacist stabbed two men to death as they tried to defend two young black women, one of whom was wearing a hijab, a traditional Muslim head covering. The attacker yelled racist things before he stabbed the men, making it clear that he was targeting the women because of their skin color and clothing. Most U.S. news outlets did not call the man a terrorist, which many experts said showed a clear double standard. Journalist Farai Chideya said, "What is terrorism? Acts designed to inspire terror. But somehow, we don't call this terrorism … When a Muslim terrorist kills one, two, five people, it's immediately labeled terrorism. But when a white nationalist kills one, two, five people, it's not labeled terrorism. But they're the same."[19] When anyone of any race or ethnicity uses biological weapons, it is an act of terrorism.

Acts of Terrorism in the United States

● left wing   ● right wing   ● Islamist

Most acts of domestic terrorism are carried out by non-Muslims, as this information from The Investigative Fund shows. This map breaks down acts of terrorism by political ideology.

The Rise of Biological Attacks

Not all that many years ago, a biological attack would have seemed far-fetched by the vast majority of Americans, something that could happen only in a movie. However, in the last few decades such attacks have actually occurred.

In the 1980s, French police found evidence that a German terrorist group called the Red Army Faction was developing biological weapons, including botulinum toxin, in a bathtub in a French apartment. These activities did not result in any injuries or deaths. Then, in 1984, a terrorist group caused large numbers of people to become gravely ill. Known as the Rajneeshees, this extremist group launched its attack in Wasco County, east of Portland, Oregon, by slipping cultures of salmonella—a microbe that causes severe food poisoning—into salad bars in 10 restaurants. Authorities counted 751 cases of the illness; fortunately, no one died in this incident.

Perhaps because there were no fatalities in the Rajneeshee attack, the media did not give the story much attention, and most of those Americans who did hear about it seem to have considered it a bizarre act perpetrated by fanatics and unlikely to be repeated. However, only six years later, in March 1990, a Japanese terrorist group called Aum Shinrikyo showed that the Rajneeshee incident was no fluke and that bioterrorism was clearly on the rise. Members of Aum Shinrikyo created masses of botulinum toxin in a secret makeshift lab. Luckily for the intended targets of the 1990 attack, the terrorists lacked the technical knowledge to properly weaponize their deadly cultures, so when they sprayed the toxin into the air at U.S. naval bases in Japan, the poison was not concentrated enough to kill anyone. Members of Aum Shinrikyo also attempted to culture anthrax bacteria and stole Ebola viruses from an African lab. If they had not been caught, they would probably have used these germs in later attacks.

In October and November 2001, letters containing deadly anthrax spores were delivered to the *New York Post*, NBC anchorman Tom Brokaw, and U.S. senators Tom Daschle and Patrick Leahy. None of these people were infected, but 22 other people contracted anthrax, 5 of whom died. Most of the victims apparently came into contact with the spores through cross-contamination, when some of the tiny particles leaked from the five envelopes while they were en route to their destinations.

4TH GRADE
GREENDALE School
FRANKLIN PARK NJ 08852

SENATOR DASCHLE
509 HART SENATE OFFICE
BUILDING
WASHINGTON D.C. 2051

20510/4103

Shown here is one of the letters containing anthrax that were sent out in 2001. These letters spread fear across the United States.

Although the death toll of these anthrax attacks was relatively low, the assaults spread fear through the entire U.S. population. This was most likely helped by the fact that the United States was already living in a climate of fear and watchfulness after September 11, 2001. For weeks after the incidents, the media reported numerous instances in which quantities of unidentified white, powdery substances were spotted in various towns and cities; local evacuations followed while teams of investigators wearing special protective suits examined the powders. Most of these events turned out to be false alarms.

Some biological attacks are small-scale and may be done to get an innocent person in trouble. For example, in 2004, someone attempted to poison children with ricin by putting pieces of castor beans into baby food jars, along with threatening notes explaining that the food was poisoned. The notes claimed that a specific police officer from Irvine, California, was responsible. The Irvine police force believed the officer was innocent and that it was an attempt to frame him for attempted murder.

An Unusual Plot

In April 2013, a letter addressed to President Barack Obama tested positive for ricin powder. Obama never received the letter because it was tested at the White House's mail processing facility, which is not located at the White House. Mail that is addressed to a president is often tested for suspicious substances there before being passed on. Ricin can be deadly if it is eaten or inhaled; if inhaled, it causes symptoms such as fever, cough, nausea, and buildup of fluid in the lungs, and if eaten, it can cause bloody diarrhea, seizures, and hallucinations. Security expert James Ramgoli told the *Los Angeles Times* that ricin poisoning is not something most people should worry about; it is not contagious—someone must come into direct contact with the substance—and it is difficult to make ricin powder so fine that it can easily float through the air.

In addition to Obama, letters were sent to Senator Roger Wicker and Mississippi judge Sadie Holland. Officials originally arrested Paul Kevin Curtis, who made his living impersonating the late singer Elvis Presley. However, after failing to find enough evidence against Curtis, they released him and arrested tae kwon do instructor James Everett Dutschke, a man who had a feud with Curtis and was apparently sending the letters to government officials in an attempt to frame Curtis. Dutschke was sentenced to 25 years in prison.

Foreign Terrorists

For the past few decades, American fears of radical Islamic terrorism have been steadily growing. In 1988, Osama bin Laden founded al-Qaeda, a radical group that rejects the traditional teachings of Islam—a religion with strict rules against suicide and killing innocent people. This group and others, including ISIS, have used Islam as an excuse to commit violent crimes, but they have also taken credit for many crimes they were later found not to have committed so they can build reputations as groups to be feared and respected. This often leads to Westerners seeing all Muslims as potential terrorists and incorrectly blaming the religion of Islam for encouraging violence.

The terrorists themselves are largely at fault for this misunderstanding of Islam, as they use its teachings in ways the vast majority of Muslims do not agree with. For instance, bin Laden declared a jihad against the United States, saying the country was a threat to Islam and that it was Muslims' duty to kill all Americans. Since then, many people have linked the word "jihad" with the idea of a violent crusade carried out for religious purposes. However, scholars of Islam say the term

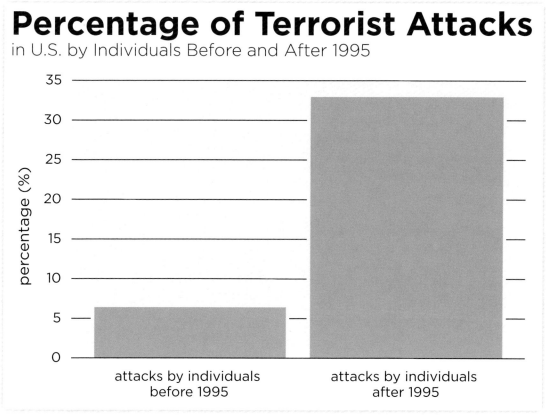

Percentage of Terrorist Attacks
in U.S. by Individuals Before and After 1995

Since 1995, terrorist attacks of all kinds have increasingly been carried out by individuals rather than groups, as this information from the Washington Post *shows.*

"literally means 'exerted effort' to most Islamic scholars and Muslims, and represents a wide range of activities."[20] According to Noha Aboulmagd-Forster, a Muslim professor, the most common interpretation of jihad for followers of Islam is a struggle for self-improvement.

Sadly, although the overwhelming majority of Muslims follow Islam's peaceful teachings, those who belong to extremist groups still pose a threat to many countries. Most of the violence they inflict is currently done with guns, traditional bombs, or by hitting people with cars at high speeds, but some news stories have pointed toward their attempts to create biological weapons. In August 2014, for instance, a laptop was recovered from an ISIS hideout and was found to contain information about weaponizing bubonic plague and other diseases. In May 2016, when an ISIS terrorist was arrested in Brussels, Belgium, officials found rotting animal parts and feces in his backpack. If he had been able to put this in a water supply, he could have made many people ill. A Brussels official stated that laboratory tests proved there was no way to weaponize the material, such as by putting it in a bomb, but some people believe this incident points to ISIS's desire to make more dangerous biological weapons.

Domestic Terrorism

Many people fear an attack from foreign terrorists, especially since these are the ones the media tends to focus on. However, the threat of domestic terrorists who might use biological weapons against their fellow citizens is no less worrisome. In fact, recent reports have found that the majority of terrorists who have attacked the United States are American right-wing extremists. Like Islamic terrorists, most of these attacks have used guns or traditional bombs as the weapon of choice, but officials have not ruled out the possibility that they might use biological weapons at some point.

The motivations of domestic bioterrorists are similar to those of their foreign counterparts in some cases. Both might want to call attention to a particular political cause they advocate and fight for, and in the view of a terrorist born and bred in America's democratic society, their biological attack might constitute a form of civic protest. This was indeed the motivation of a domestic terrorist group calling itself the Patriots Council. In 1994, the group planned to protest against what it saw as unfair U.S. tax laws by using ricin toxin to kill several U.S. agents. The culprits were captured, however, before they could put their plan into action.

DOMESTIC TERRORISM SHOULD NOT BE IGNORED

"First thing we need to do is recognize that [far-right extremism is] there, it's a problem, it's a threat—as great a threat as Islamists ... And it needs to be taken seriously."

–David Neiwert, lead reporter of a joint terrorism study by the Nation Institute and the Center for Investigative Reporting

Quoted in Sarah Ruiz-Grossman, "Most of America's Terrorists Are White, and Not Muslim," *Huffington Post*, June 23, 2017. www.huffingtonpost.com/entry/domestic-terrorism-white-supremacists-islamist-extremists_us_594c46e4e4b0da2c731a84df.

Other common motives of domestic bioterrorists are best described as religious or racist. The two are often linked because many who claim they possess racial superiority believe their ideology is ordained and sanctioned by God. Such feelings of racial and religious superiority were behind a planned domestic bio-attack in 1972. Two members of an extreme right-wing group called R.I.S.E., who wanted to promote a white master race, were arrested in Chicago, Illinois. They were in possession of several pounds of typhoid fever cultures with which they were going to poison the city's water supply. Three years later, members of an extreme left-wing group, the Symbionese Liberation Army, were caught with technical manuals on how to manufacture bioweapons.

Still another potential cause of domestic biological terrorist attacks is what experts call the copycat phenomenon. In such cases, would-be terrorists are inspired by and want to imitate antisocial and criminal acts perpetrated by other terrorists. A well-documented example occurred in the 1990s. In 1995,

Larry Wayne Harris, a member of a white supremacist group, purchased three vials containing bubonic plague bacteria and some considerable quantities of anthrax bacteria. His reasons for doing this were never reported, but authorities suspected he wanted to use them as biological weapons. They arrested him in 1998 before he could use these deadly agents, but for nearly a year after news of his aborted attack was released, other copycats imitated Harris by issuing threats to launch their own anthrax attacks or staging hoaxes designed to make it look as if they had done so.

Entomological Warfare

Entomological warfare is a type of biological warfare that uses insects to spread disease. Like the use of germs and toxins, it has been around for a relatively long time. After World War II, the United States conducted research that created yellow fever-carrying mosquitoes, which could have infected thousands of people if the mosquitoes had been released. During the Cold War, Cuba accused the United States of using insects to spread dengue fever and bugs that would eat important crops, although those accusations were never proven. Another unproven accusation was made during the Korean War, when North Korea and China accused the United States of using flies and mosquitoes to spread germs.

Although it is possible to release disease-carrying insects, it is very difficult for anyone to prove it was done deliberately. According to University of Wyoming professor Jeffrey Lockwood, "You don't really notice the infestation until it's well underway ... Distinguishing accident from intention, especially with something like a crop pest, is darn near impossible."[1] However, experts say the average person should not worry about entomological warfare, since the BWC outlawed the use of bugs as weapons along with other biological agents.

1. Quoted in Stephanie Merry, "The Insect Warfare on 'The Americans' Isn't All That Outlandish," Washington Post, March 22, 2017. www.washingtonpost.com/news/arts-and-entertainment/wp/2017/03/22/the-insect-warfare-on-the-americans-isnt-all-that-outlandish/?utm_term=.3da4e2002e20.

Sometimes the acts of domestic terrorists are falsely blamed on foreign terrorists. When the letters containing anthrax were mailed after September 11, nearly everyone suspected al-Qaeda because the two attacks came so close together. The FBI investigated, and almost immediately, investigators learned from the evidence that the letters were written by an American who was trying to impersonate an Islamic extremist. However, many people remained unaware of this fact and continued to blame foreign terrorists.

In 2010, the FBI announced the true culprit. It was revealed that the man behind these attacks was not a foreign terrorist but was actually Dr. Bruce Ivins, a white microbiologist who worked for the U.S. Army. According to the criminal report, "Dr. Ivins embedded in the notes mailed with the anthrax a complex coded message, based on DNA biochemistry, alluding to two female former colleagues with whom he was obsessed."[21]

Although the exact motives of domestic bioterrorists vary, experts recognize one important factor all terrorists—domestic and foreign—have in common: Both individual terrorists and the leaders and followers of terrorist groups are attracted to violence for its own sake. They then try to rationalize their fascination with violence. They do this by saying that violent acts are the only way to achieve their stated political, religious, social, or racist goals.

Bruce Ivins (shown here) was found to have mailed the anthrax letters after 9/11. He committed suicide in 2008, but the investigation was ongoing until 2010.

FEAR IGNORES REALITY

"Biological weapons are widely viewed with dread,
though in actual use they have rarely done great harm."

—Gregg Easterbrook, journalist

Gregg Easterbrook, "The Meaninglessness of Term Limits," *New Republic*, October 7, 2002.

The Threat of Agroterrorism

Another kind of bioterrorist attack against the United States that experts say could happen in the future is an agroterrorist attack. As terrorism expert Anne Kohnen wrote,

> Agricultural targets are "soft targets," or ones that maintain such a low level of security that a terrorist could carry out an attack unobserved. Biological agents are small, inexpensive, and nearly impossible to detect. A terrorist may choose to use [bioweapons] against agriculture simply because it is the easiest and cheapest way to cause large-scale damage.[22]

Kohnen and other experts point out that besides being easy and cheap, agroterrorism may be attractive for those few terrorists who retain some moral constraints. In other words, a recruit who is reluctant to directly kill many humans might have few or no moral qualms about inflicting economic damage on the United States by destroying crops and livestock. Another advantage for the attackers would be anonymity. Experts acknowledge that unless the agroterrorists were sloppy in their efforts, finding them would be nearly impossible.

There is no doubt that a successful agroterrorist attack against the United States could be potentially devastating. In the late 1990s, Belgium suffered a terrorist assault in which someone placed dioxin, a harmful chemical, in local chicken feed. That nation's economy suffered an estimated $1 billion in losses as a result. In addition to causing fear and panic, a single agroterrorist attack in the United States, some experts estimate, could cost the country $100 billion or more. According to a 2003 report by the RAND Corporation, a nonprofit research organization, "A major agroterrorist attack would have substantial economic repercussions, especially when allied industries and services—suppliers, transporters, distributors, and restaurant chains—are taken into account."[23] The report pointed out several reasons why agricultural companies are especially vulnerable:

- Farms often crowd animals close together, so a disease would spread quickly among livestock.

- The way animals have been raised for meat has made them less able to fight off disease; for instance, many livestock companies overuse antibiotics, which makes the bacteria stronger over time.

- Livestock producers may hide the fact that some of their animals are sick so their profits do not go down. The longer they hide it, the worse the problem would become.

Agroterrorism could have terrible effects on the economy and food supply of the United States.

- Many veterinarians are unfamiliar with foreign livestock diseases.

- Livestock producers with large herds may not notice if one or two animals are sick, which gives a disease a better chance of spreading.

Although the threat of a biological attack seems worrisome, officials have spent years coming up with ways to fight these attacks.

Fighting Biological Attacks

Health officials in the United States have spent years studying biological agents to determine the best way to defend against them. Most of this research is top secret to avoid giving terrorists or rogue states information about the best way to attack. However, to reassure the public and reinforce trust in the government, they have let certain things be known. These include emergency plans to handle sudden outbreaks of disease; stepped-up security in office buildings, sports stadiums, and other places where large numbers of people gather; drills staged periodically to prepare first responders such as police, firefighters, contagious disease experts, and medical personnel for emergencies; expansion of the resources of public health departments to make them better able to respond to a biological attack; the manufacture of large amounts of existing vaccines that might need to be administered to millions of citizens following a major biological attack; and other related measures.

Some progress has definitely been made in each of these areas since 2001 in the United States and other industrialized nations. However, as technology advances, terrorists' ability to create different types of biological weapons also increases. Thus, building up defenses against potential biological attacks must be an ongoing effort. Although strides have been made in recent years, there are still some areas in which improvement is needed.

Planning and Training

Government leaders and agencies stand at the forefront of the efforts to build up both national and local defenses against biological weapons. It is the responsibility of these leaders and agencies to make public policy related to the problem. More specifically, government organizations are responsible for putting emergency plans into place. One important aspect of such plans, of course, is notifying first responders and the public of the emergency. A number of warning systems, old and new, exist for this purpose. Among them are the National Warning System (NAWAS) and Emergency Broadcast System (EBS).

Too Much Regulation Harms Trust

Since September 11, 2001, a number of states have proposed changing health laws and other laws to give state officials more power to prevent biological and other attacks. Twila Brase, president of the Citizen's Council for Health Freedom in St. Paul, Minnesota, argued that giving state governments too much power might threaten civil liberties and make the citizens angry:

> Public trust requires thoughtful contingency plans that uphold constitutional rights and freedom of conscience, support medical ethics, and encourage voluntary cooperation with disease containment strategies. State legislatures should not rush to enact ill-conceived, ineffective legislation. Public policy must always recognize and respect the rights, dignity, and intelligence of individuals. An angry public is not a cooperative public. If health officials are empowered to harm the very people legislators want to protect, a public health emergency may soon become a crisis of the public's trust.[1]

1. Twila Brase, "A Model for Medical Tyranny," Foundation for Economic Education, August 1, 2002. fee.org/articles/a-model-for-medical-tyranny/

Government officials acknowledge that warnings are merely a first step. Once notified of the emergency, trained first responders must speed into action and follow plans designed to contain or neutralize the threat. These plans are periodically reviewed and changed if necessary. For example, in March 2017, the United States Department of Agriculture (USDA) issued a report called *Agroterrorism Prevention, Detection, and Response.* The report stated that an inspection of the USDA's Office of

Homeland Security and Emergency Coordination (OHSEC) found that OHSEC could be doing a better job of stopping agroterrorism before it starts. The report recommended 14 ways OHSEC could improve—for instance, by communicating with other agencies about the ways they prevent agroterrorism. In August 2017, lawmakers met to discuss issues such as how to vaccinate animals quickly and effectively in the event of an outbreak. Additionally, in May 2017, a law called the Securing Our Agriculture and Food Act was passed giving the Department of Homeland Security (DHS) more oversight in agricultural and veterinary businesses.

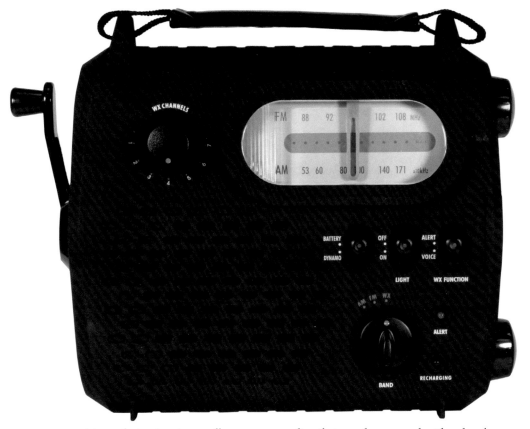

Many electronics stores sell emergency radios that can be powered with a hand crank. Important information is often broadcast through the radio, and the electricity sometimes goes out in emergency situations. As such, an emergency radio can be a useful way to find out what is going on in the event of a biological attack.

Practicing a Response

Local law enforcement officers, firefighters, public officials, and medical personnel constitute the first line of defense because they are the ones who will likely recognize the outbreak of disease or mass poisoning if and when it occurs. These individuals will also be among the initial first responders. They will secure various public buildings and sites in hopes of containing the outbreak, call in trained medical and military teams if necessary to help any victims, and begin identifying and arresting the attackers.

Since the September 11 attacks, the U.S. government has allocated extra funds to these first responders. Some of this money has been used for live drills. Since the United States has faced the possibility of a biological attack, communities across the country have developed response plans so they can quickly deal with such an event. These plans are often rehearsed the way fire drills are so they can be carried out as quickly and efficiently as possible when the emergency is real. Some drills are small; volunteers in a community may gather for a few hours on a weekend to practice distributing medicine and keeping people calm. Others are quite large. For instance, in August 2014, New York City held an anthrax drill that involved 1,500 workers from 12 city agencies. The employees practiced setting up emergency medicine distribution sites around the city to see how quickly they could get the anti-anthrax medication to the public.

One of the first drills, which was held in June 2001, demonstrated how far the United States had to go to improve its emergency measures. Large numbers of public officials and first responders around the country took part in Operation Dark Winter, a bioterrorist attack simulation—a computer program similar to a video game that showed experts how their choices would affect the aftermath of a biological attack. Although the simulation only took two days to complete, the scenario that played out in the simulation spanned about two weeks. It was designed and overseen by four leading biological warfare experts—Tara O'Toole and Thomas Inglesby of the Johns Hopkins

Since the September 11 attacks, many cities have held anthrax drills similar to the one shown here to practice handing out medication in a quick and orderly way.

Center for Civilian Biodefense Strategies, and Randy Larsen and Mark DeMier of the organization ANSER (Advancing National Strategies and Enabling Results). In the simulation, agents from a rogue nation secretly spread smallpox germs in shopping malls, and the disease spread alarmingly quickly. At the end of the first simulated day alone, 34 cases of smallpox were detected in Oklahoma, 9 in Georgia, and 7 in Pennsylvania. By the 6th simulated day, there were 2,000 cases of smallpox in 15 states, and hospitals were overwhelmed. At the end of the second simulated week, 1,000 victims were dead, the disease had spread to other countries, and medical officials predicted 3 million cases of smallpox and the loss of 1 million lives in the following 3 months.

Most of the U.S. government officials, politicians, medical personnel, and first responders who took part in this drill were genuinely surprised by its grim outcome. According to Frank Keating, a participant in the study, "We think an enemy of the United States could attack us with smallpox or with anthrax—whatever—and we really don't prepare for it, we have no vaccines for it—that's astonishing." Participant James Woolsey added, "It isn't just [a matter of] buying more vaccine. It's a question of how we integrate these [public health and national security communities] in ways that allow us to deal with various facets of the problem."[24]

VACCINATION PROGRAMS

"From a national security perspective, preemptive but voluntary smallpox vaccinations for the general public—along with a more comprehensive vaccination for military personnel and critical first responders—makes the most sense."

—Michael Scardaville, former policy analyst

Michael Scardaville, "Public Health and National Security Planning: The Case for Voluntary Smallpox Vaccination," The Heritage Foundation, December 6, 2002. www.heritage.org/homeland-security/report/public-health-and-national-security-planning-the-case-forvoluntary.

Creating a Plan

Although it is important for government officials to have a response plan in case of a biological attack, it is equally important for individuals to stay informed. It does not matter how many emergency medical sites officials are able to set up if people do not know where they are and how to get to them. The CDC encourages families to take several basic precautions, including:

- Pack an emergency supply kit that includes at least three days' worth of food and water as well as basic tools, safety and health supplies, and toiletries.

- Make sure all family members know how to contact each other and where to gather in event of an emergency.

- Determine escape routes from the house, and practice using them.

- Know who will take care of pets; some emergency shelters do not allow them.

- Know which TV and radio stations to tune to for emergency alerts.

- Know where to go if you need to get emergency medication.

- Keep up-to-date family medical information handy so doctors know the right medication and dosage to give everyone.

The Effects on Health Care Workers

Though public officials and planners play a central role in preparing to deal with potential biological crises, diagnosing the initial victims, curing them, and trying to keep the disease from spreading will be the job of doctors, nurses, paramedics, and other trained health personnel. David Stipp, a science writer for *Fortune* magazine, wrote, "The horrible burden [of being the first line of defense] will fall on hospitals and public health agencies that are hard-pressed even to handle their everyday workloads."[25]

Indeed, though the vast majority of public health personnel are skilled and dedicated, they themselves recognize that the present resources and training they possess may be inadequate in a real biological warfare emergency. The Institute of Medicine of the National Academies wrote about this issue in 2007:

> *The day before September 11, 2001, the cover story of* U.S. News and World Report *described an emergency care system in critical condition as a result of demand far in excess of its capacity ... While the article focused on the day-to-day problems of diversion and boarding, the events of the following day brought home a frightening realization to many. If we cannot take care of our emergency patients on a normal day, how will we manage a large-scale disaster? Federal, state, and local government entities have since realized the importance of hospitals, particularly emergency departments (EDs), in planning for such events, and significant progress has been made on integrating inpatient resources into planning for disasters.*[26]

Another concern that has been raised is that many doctors and nurses might not initially recognize that a disease they were seeing in their emergency rooms had been spread by malicious attackers. Indeed, "it is doubtful that anyone would notice," expert Barbara F. Bullock commented,

> *that the influx of patients currently being treated in multiple emergency facilities came from the same geographical area. The patients would be treated by another set of physicians who are even less likely ... to recognize the symptoms*

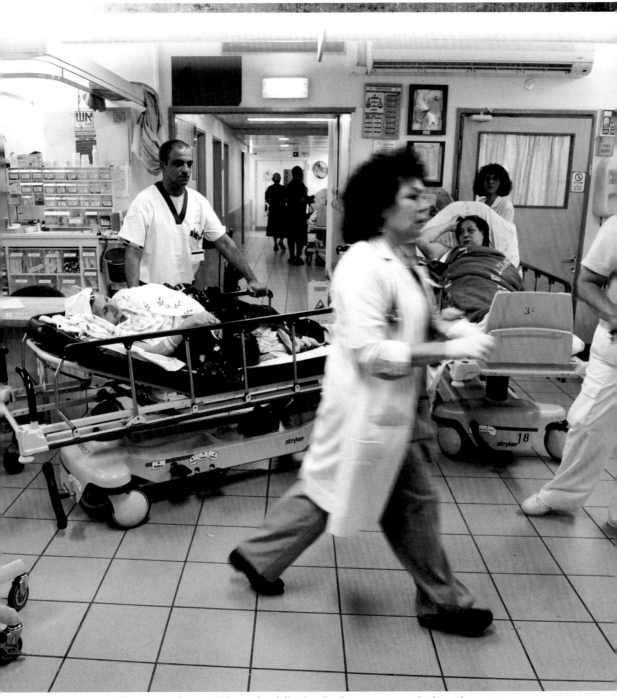

Health care workers will have the difficult job of recognizing a biological agent's symptoms and, if the disease is contagious, keeping it from spreading.

that manifest from exposure to biological attacks, since few [modern] physicians have seen a case of anthrax, smallpox, or the plague.[27]

To try to address some of these problems, 49 New York City hospitals participated in a "mystery patient" drill between December 2015 and May 2016, in which a patient exhibiting symptoms of a highly contagious disease such as measles entered an emergency room. Most of the staff were unaware that the patient was secretly perfectly healthy. The drill tested how quickly staff assessed the patient's symptoms, gave them a mask to prevent infecting others, and put them in an isolation room. A drill was considered failed if the patient waited more than 30 minutes for medical attention, if the staff did not correctly identify a possibly contagious disease, or if proper procedures were not followed—for example, if the patient was not offered a mask. There were 95 drills conducted, and 19 out of 49 hospitals—39 percent of the participants—failed at least 1 drill. These results allow professionals to create better training programs for hospitals.

It has also been demonstrated that few diagnostic laboratories in the United States possess the resources to rapidly confirm the presence of these otherwise rare diseases. As a result of these deficiencies, Bullock and other experts have called for the installation of improved laboratory instruments and more and better training of medical personnel to recognize a biological attack when it occurs. Other suggestions for improvement include developing new, cutting-edge diagnostic tools that could identify the presence of biological agents within 30 minutes; organizing special teams of doctors and nurses who could respond to biological attacks quickly and efficiently; creating new plans to coordinate these responders and other health care professionals with state and federal public officials; and stockpiling vaccines to safeguard human and animal populations from the spread of diseases caused by biological agents.

The Use of Medications

Vaccines and antibiotics are among the most important tools used by health care professionals to combat diseases spread during biological attacks. Antibiotics are helpful after someone has been infected, especially in the case of anthrax. If someone gets the medication quickly enough, it could save their life. Vaccines, however, are a more complicated subject.

There is no doubt that vaccines can be effective in preventing or fighting disease epidemics. However, according to Philip K. Russell of Johns Hopkins School of Public Health, using vaccines to protect a large population from a biological attack is more difficult than many people think. The biological agent would have to be identified before the vaccine could be given, which might take some time. Vaccines are also expensive, and although members of the military are vaccinated against biological agents such as smallpox and anthrax, most health officials agree that it is a waste of time and money to vaccinate everyone when the risk of someone creating a biological weapon that can effectively infect hundreds of people is quite small. The best use of vaccines in a biological attack, according to Russell, would be to give them to first responders such as hospital and laboratory workers so they can work on containing the disease without getting sick themselves.

Another aspect of the issue is that vaccines are only effective if the person receives them before they contract the disease, so health officials would have to work incredibly quickly both to contain the disease and to vaccinate people before it spreads. Sometimes this may not be possible. The existing vaccine for anthrax is a case in point. It is generally effective, and tens of thousands of U.S. service personnel have received it thus far. However, it requires five separate inoculations, plus boosters each subsequent year. This means that if the anthrax is not well contained, people may not be able to receive all five vaccines before they come in contact with it.

Vaccinating against smallpox in particular is generally considered not only unnecessary, but dangerous. Experts insist

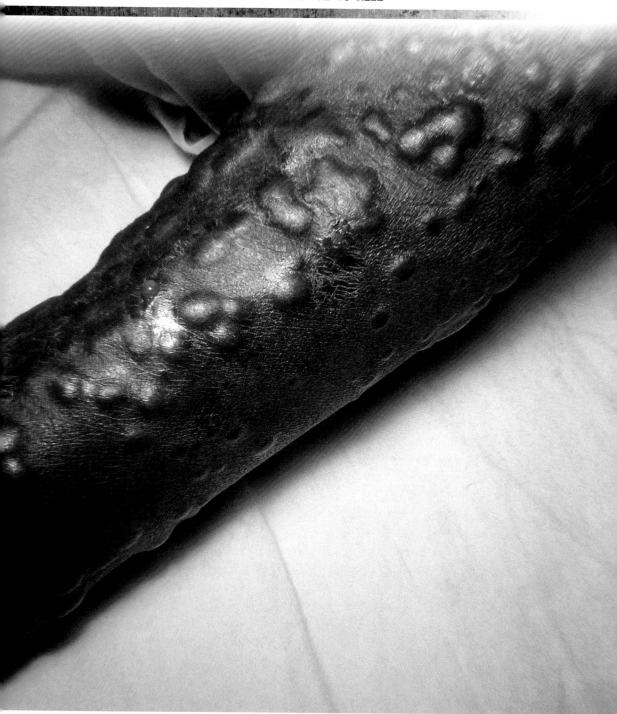

Shown here is what the arm of a person infected with smallpox looks like.

that mass smallpox vaccinations before any biological attack had occurred would waste precious resources and unnecessarily scare citizens. In addition, the vaccination programs could end up killing people. In 2002, *60 Minutes II* reported that the smallpox vaccine is known to be dangerous and that the government did not recommend anyone except military personnel get it. According to Steven Black of Cincinnati Children's Hospital,

> One out of 500,000 individuals will die as a direct cause of the vaccine. Although the risk of either death or … severe side effects may sound relatively rare, vaccination of the entire U.S. population would result in 600 deaths and 2,000 individuals with serious brain infections. These very real risks must be balanced against what is currently only a theoretical risk of smallpox being introduced by terrorists.[28]

Although the vaccine is dangerous, the disease is much worse; people in an area where smallpox had been released would have a choice of potentially dying from the vaccine or certainly dying from the disease. For this reason, Black added that localized smallpox vaccinations in specific areas would be sensible after a confirmed biological attack in those regions. Thus, vaccines may prove to be important tools in biodefense efforts even if mass inoculations on a national scale are never employed.

Quarantine and Isolation Laws

According to a number of experts and public officials, reforming and streamlining public health laws is another potential tool in biodefense efforts. However, the idea of making major changes in U.S. public health laws remains more controversial than most people realize. Some experts point out that these laws are outmoded and need to be changed to make them work better against potential bioterrorists. In fact, according to Lawrence O. Gostin, who teaches public health at Johns Hopkins University, "Public-health laws across the country are highly antiquated [out of date], built up in layers during the last century."[29]

These laws generally regulate who can be quarantined or isolated, for what reasons, and for how long. Quarantine means anyone who may have potentially been exposed to a disease must remain separated from people until it can be determined whether they have been infected. Isolation means keeping a person who is known or suspected to be infected separate until they are no longer contagious. Both federal and state governments have the power to quarantine or isolate people. The federal government is also able, in certain extreme circumstances, to make temporary laws restricting travel to prevent the spread of a disease. For instance, it may shut down public transportation or ban people from driving across state lines until it seems like the danger of transmitting the disease has passed.

A LAST RESORT

"Unfortunately, the smallpox vaccine is just not as safe as any of the other vaccines routinely used in the United States today."

–Steven Black, journalist

Steven Black, "Smallpox Sense," *Vaccination News*, accessed September 6, 2017. www.vaccinationnews.org/Scandals/Feb_8_02/SmallVaxRisks.htm.

Some experts feel the laws should be strengthened to give the government greater control in the event of a biological attack. For instance, in 2001, Gostin proposed the Model State Emergency Health Powers Act (MSEHPA). It granted state governments extreme power in the event of a public health emergency, such as the ability to quarantine anyone or seize their property if they are suspected of having a disease that is a threat to public health.

Some people approved of MSEHPA; while the total law was not passed, many states passed bills that were similar to some parts of MSEHPA. However, other experts and concerned citizens see major changes in the nation's health laws as unwise because they might pose a threat to civil liberties. In particular, these individuals worry that changes in the laws might grant too much power to state governors and the leading health officials working under them. MSEHPA would give these officials the authority to force many citizens to give up their privacy, or even control over their own bodies, in the name of public safety. The American Civil Liberties Union (ACLU) opposed the act for multiple reasons:

> Public health authorities make mistakes, and politicians abuse their powers; there is a history of discriminatory use of the quarantine power against particular groups of people based on race and national origin, for example ... The Act lets a governor declare a state of emergency [without consulting other officials and] fails to provide modern due process procedures for quarantine and other emergency powers, it lacks adequate compensation for seizure of assets, and contains no checks on the power to order forced treatment and vaccination ...
>
> The Act requires the disclosure of massive amounts of personally identifiable health information to public health authorities, without requiring basic privacy protections and fair information practices that could easily be added to the bill without detracting from its effectiveness in quelling an outbreak. And the Model Act would undercut existing protections for sensitive medical information. That not only threatens to violate individuals' medical privacy but undermines public trust in government activities.[30]

The ACLU and others believe laws can be strengthened without harming civil liberties, but many laws that are proposed do not take this into account. For example, during the Ebola scare of 2014, at least six states issued tougher regulations for people returning from trips to places where Ebola is more common. In one case, nurse Kaci Hickox was held against her will for six hours at Newark Liberty International Airport in New Jersey. She had been treating Ebola patients in the country of Sierra Leone in Africa, but she showed no symptoms and tested negative for the disease twice. Additionally, people who

Kaci Hickox (shown here) was held against her will at Newark Airport even though she tested negative for Ebola and showed no symptoms.

are infected are not contagious until symptoms appear, and the disease is difficult to catch. For these reasons, many people disagreed with New Jersey's decision to essentially hold her captive for those six hours, feeling that the response was a severe overreaction to a situation that was not actually dangerous. These people oppose laws that would give states the power to do this in other circumstances.

This debate about changing health care laws to better deal with the threat of biological attacks, such as the issue of mass vaccinations, demonstrates that preparation for and appropriate public responses to such attacks are far from simple and obvious. Indeed, they are complex issues relating to individual privacy, civil liberties, personal and public safety, and the proper role of government in the lives of citizens in an open democracy. Some people advocate doing whatever seems necessary to protect the public from harm, even if some freedoms must be sacrificed. They sometimes use the phrase, "The Constitution is not a suicide pact," which paraphrases a similar statement made by Supreme Court Justice Robert H. Jackson in 1949, when he argued that some restrictions on civil liberties are needed to keep the general public safe. Others disagree and repeat a famous quote attributed to one of America's Founding Fathers, Benjamin Franklin: "They who would give up essential liberty to purchase a little temporary safety, deserve neither liberty or safety."[31] It appears that few, if any, of these contentious issues will be resolved until the United States or another nation faces one or more large-scale biological attacks. Such events, if they ever do happen, will force those in charge to make definite decisions one way or another.

CHAPTER 5

Preparing for the Future

The threat of biological warfare may not be immediate, but it does exist, and experts agree it is better to be prepared than to wait until something happens. Technology will likely open up new, deadly means for making and delivering biological agents, and for this reason, researchers are already looking for ways to detect and combat these potential new weapons.

The natural question is: How will governments and citizens deal with these new and frightening challenges, as well as with existing biological warfare challenges? More specifically, how can these threats be prevented in the first place? Although there is no single or simple answer to these questions, various scientists, military strategists, politicians, and other experts have offered suggestions. Among them are stricter adherence to international conventions banning the use of weapons of mass destruction, the use of nuclear weapons as a counterthreat to bioweapons, improving biodefenses through medical and technical advances, and setting strong moral standards for all nations and individuals to follow.

Discussing an Enforcement Protocol

In regard to international conventions and protocols, the major nations of the world have been legally bound by the articles of the BWC since 1975, the year it officially went into effect. This does not mean, however, that all the signers of the convention obeyed the rules and refrained from making new biological weapons. As a result, a number of national leaders and expert observers came to view the BWC as basically useless.

Biological Warfare and Science Fiction

Biological weapons have been a source of fascination for writers and readers for many years. One famous example is *War of the Worlds* by H.G. Wells, in which invading aliens are defeated by human germs they have no resistance to, such as the common cold. Some stories involve realistic scenarios and known biological agents, while others invent things that are not currently possible, such as a virus that could hide inside a human body until an attacker uses a certain chemical or sound frequency to activate it. A biological agent is also frequently used as an explanation in fiction about zombies. The website TV Tropes described several points that are common to most biological warfare stories:

It can go by many names: The "Virus", The "Plague", The "Cure", The "Cleansing", etc, but it fits the same criteria:

1. *It targets only living things. Infrastructure and biospheres are left untouched.*

2. *It will completely destroy the enemy ranks, or at least decimate them to the point that they are not a significant threat.*

3. *It can be spread across the entire kingdom, continent, planet, universe, etc.*

4. *It has a half-life long enough or communicability rapid enough that it's nigh-impossible to escape.*

5. *(Optional) It will target the enemy and only the enemy, leaving the deploying army free from consequence.*[1]

Biological attacks are a common trope in science fiction stories.

1. "Biological Weapons Solve Everything," TV Tropes, accessed August 30, 2017. tvtropes.org/pmwiki/pmwiki.php/Main/BiologicalWeaponsSolveEverything.

However, some of these critics recognized that the BWC and other such international agreements retained at least the potential for reducing the creation of weapons of mass destruction. The problem, the critics pointed out, was that the BWC lacked provisions for enforcing its will; in other words, the signers of the treaty could not legally force a suspected rule breaker to allow international inspections and investigations of its labs and other facilities. In the 1990s, therefore, a group of diplomats from several countries began drawing up a special enforcement protocol they hoped to add to the BWC. Completed in April 2001, the protocol provided for a unit of inspectors to monitor the biological research activities of BWC members.

Nuclear Weapons Are Not the Answer

General Lee Butler, former commander of the U.S. Strategic Air Command, argued that any faith that nuclear weapons will deter the use of biological weapons is misplaced:

> Sad to say, the Cold War lives on in the minds of those who cannot let go the fears, beliefs, and the enmities born of the nuclear age. What better illustration of misplaced faith in nuclear deterrence than the persistent belief that the retaliation with nuclear weapons is a legitimate and appropriate response to post-Cold War threats posed by biological ... weapons of mass destruction ... What could possibly justify our resorting to the very means we properly abhor and condemn? ... Would we hold an entire society accountable for the decision of a single demented leader? ... It is wrong in every aspect. It is wrong politically. It makes no sense militarily. And morally, in my view, it is indefensible.[1]

1. Lee Butler, "The Case Against Nuclear Deterrence," *Disarmament Times*, April 1998.

Several countries declared their willingness to sign the new protocol. However, the United States refused to sign. The administration of President George W. Bush claimed it could not accept the protocol because the rules set forth in the document are too weak to catch potential cheaters. Both the administration and supporters of its rejection of the protocol also said that some of the provisions of the document might reveal vital military secrets and this could potentially pose a risk to U.S. national security.

Those critical of the refusal of the United States to accept the new protocol pointed to what they viewed as the document's potential benefits. They also said the refusal makes the United States look less reasonable than several nations widely viewed as rogue states. However, the United States held firm.

Some experts believe there are other ways to strengthen the BWC. In 2011, Kay Mereish, deputy director of the Department of Homeland Security at the National Center for Medical Intelligence, proposed several alternatives, such as encouraging cooperation and interaction between countries so they have less incentive to use biological weapons against each other.

Using Nuclear Weapons as a Threat

Some of the same experts who oppose U.S. acceptance of the BWC Protocol think that at least some future biological attacks may be prevented by nuclear deterrence. In other words, someone may refrain from launching a biological attack out of fear of nuclear retaliation. Experts caution that if this kind of deterrence works at all, it will likely work mainly in the specific case of rogue nations rather than that of individual terrorists or terrorist groups. Terrorists will probably not be deterred by a nuclear threat because they do not generally represent or act on the orders of an organized nation.

A rogue nation-state, on the other hand, may be deterred by a nuclear response if it is proven to be behind a deadly attack on another country, so the leader or leaders of such a state may think twice about launching biological weapons against a nuclear power such as the United States, Russia, Britain, or Israel.

BIODEFENSE IN THE 21ST CENTURY

"Defending against biological weapons attacks requires us to further sharpen our policy, coordination, and planning to integrate the biodefense capabilities that reside at the Federal, state, local, and private sector levels."

–George W. Bush, 43rd President of the United States

George W. Bush, "Biodefense for the 21st Century," in *Homeland Security: Protecting America's Targets*, ed. James J.F. Forest. Westport, CT: Praeger, 2006, p. 434.

For this reason, some experts say the United States should keep the threat of nuclear retaliation as a sort of trump card against potential future biological attacks by rogue nations such as North Korea. According to David G. Gompert,

> While it is possible to imagine a biological attack that would not warrant a nuclear response, this is no reason to discard the option of a nuclear response against any and all possible biological attacks. When thousands of Soviet nuclear weapons were poised to strike, the first use of nuclear weapons by the United States risked a general nuclear cataclysm. In contrast, U.S. nuclear retaliation for a biological attack by a rogue state would risk, at worst, another [biological or chemical] attack—awful to be sure, but worth the risk in order to deter biological use in the first place. More likely, having proven its resolve with a presumably selective nuclear detonation, the United States would deter further escalation and prevail.[32]

However, not everyone agrees that nuclear weapons are the answer. Some worry about unnecessary nuclear proliferation. They say that if the few existing nuclear powers begin using their nuclear bombs to deter biological or chemical attacks, many other nations will decide they need nuclear weapons for the same purpose. Former U.S. diplomat Thomas Graham Jr. declared,

> Nuclear deterrence is ill-suited to protecting the United States and its interests against ... biological attacks, and to employ it in this fashion would make the spread of nuclear weapons much

Some people believe a large stockpile of nuclear weapons similar to the missiile shown here will deter terrorists from using biological weapons. Others do not agree.

more likely. We can deter and respond to ... biological weapons in a manner fully protective of our national security; we cannot assure our national security in a world armed to the teeth with nuclear weapons.[33]

Others believe nuclear weapons are not a deterrent at all. It was commonly believed during the Cold War that the Soviet Union and the United States did not attack each other only because they knew the other had nuclear weapons, but in recent years, people have begun to question this view. As history professor Lawrence Wittner pointed out, "since 1945, many nations not in possession of nuclear weapons and not part of the alliance systems of the nuclear powers have not experienced a military attack. Clearly, they survived just fine without nuclear deterrence."[34] He went on to point out that the U.S. stockpile of nuclear weapons did not stop China from attacking U.S. troops in the Korean War or prevent the attacks on September 11, 2001, from happening. Wittner and others believe the possession of nuclear weapons is not enough of a threat to prevent a biological attack from other countries. Additionally, they would be useless against a domestic terrorist such as Bruce Ivins.

Policy Changes

As technology improves, terrorists and rogue states have more options for creating effective biological weapons. One concern experts have is the rise of genetic engineering. By using relatively inexpensive home gene-editing kits, terrorists could theoretically alter the deoxyribonucleic acid (DNA) of a virus or bacterium. DNA is the substance in all living things that determines their individual characteristics. If a terrorist discovered a way to change the DNA of a microorganism to make it more powerful, more infectious, or more resistant to current medications, a biological attack could become more deadly. Genetic engineering could also allow someone to bring back a disease that has been eradicated, such as polio or smallpox. In February 2017, Bill Gates, the founder of Microsoft, "warned that a conflict involving such weapons could kill more people than nuclear war."[35] Because of this fear, many people feel the United States should concentrate its resources on biodefense, and in 2016, Congress passed the National Defense Authorization Act, which requires the federal government to develop a plan for biodefense. Some have also encouraged the administration of President Donald Trump to assign a specific person, such as the vice president, to work on biodefense so there is no confusion about policy.

Experts say more funding for laboratories would help prepare the United States for a possible biological attack.

A number of experts also say that simply providing more government funding would allow the building of more and better lab facilities. At present, they say, not enough labs in the United States and other Western countries are equipped with the latest devices for recognizing and culturing some of the germs that rogue states or terrorists might use in an attack. At the same time, these experts say, existing computer databases should be expanded to provide support in diagnosing and treating diseases released by attackers. Tom Ridge, the first Secretary of Homeland Security, and former senator Joseph Lieberman "urge Congress to implement uniform budgeting and build preparedness measures into annual budgets, instead of relying on emergency funding bills that cost lives and financial resources."[36] They also recommended that the 20 Congressional committees that currently oversee biodefense be combined into one or two so they do not lose time fighting over who should take action when a problem occurs.

Technological Advancements

Attackers are not the only ones taking advantage of technology; scientists are doing so as well. In 2013, researchers created a cube called SpinDx that can test liquids such as blood, vomit, and even water for the presence of biological agents. SpinDx needs only a tiny sample of liquid, and it can give results in as little as 15 minutes. *Popular Science* reported on the capabilities of SpinDx, stating that botulism in particular is "a difficult disease to test for—current standard practice requires a test on live mice. According to Sandia National Laboratories researcher Greg Sommer, the SpinDx test 'vastly outperformed the mouse bioassay in head-to-head tests, and requires absolutely no animal testing.'"[37]

Other researchers are working on fighting microorganisms with microorganisms. At Johns Hopkins University, scientists are trying to engineer two types of bacteria to find and destroy other bacteria before they infect people. However, the project is concentrating on bacteria outside the human body; rather than putting the engineered bacteria into people like a vaccine, the researchers hope to be able to release their disease-fighting bacteria into the air to neutralize diseases before people catch them. Specifically, they are focusing on releasing them into hospital air vents; people in hospitals are generally less able to fight off diseases, which is why hospitals keep everything sterile, or germ-free. This may make hospitals a target for a biological attack.

Scientists in other countries are also working on ways to fight bioterrorism. In South Korea, researchers at the Korea Advanced Institute of Science and Technology trained artificial intelligence (AI) to spot anthrax in less than 1 second, with 96 percent accuracy. The faster anthrax can be identified, the sooner officials can contain it and treat anyone who came into contact with it. The current method involves scientists analyzing the spores themselves, which takes at least a day because if the sample is small, they must let it grow so they have enough material to test. This seems like a short amount of time, but since anthrax can kill an infected person in as little as one day, it is too long. *The Verge* explained what the South Korean scientists did:

> [Physicist YongKeun Park] *turned to an imaging technique called holographic microscopy: unlike conventional microscopes, which can only capture the intensity of the light scattering off an object, a holographic microscope can also capture the direction that light is traveling. Since the structure and makeup of a cell can change how light bounces off of it, the researchers suspected that the holographic microscope might capture key, but subtle, differences between spores produced by anthrax and those produced by closely related, but less toxic species …*
>
> *Park and his team then trained a deep learning algorithm to spot these key differences in more than 400 individual spores from five different species of bacteria. One species was* Bacillus anthracis, *which causes anthrax, and four were closely related doppelgängers. The researchers didn't tell the neural network exactly how to spot the differences—the AI figured that out on its own. After some training, it could distinguish the anthrax spores from the non-anthrax doppelgänger species about 96 percent of the time.*[38]

The next step will be for researchers to work on improving the AI's accuracy. Although 96 percent is nearly perfect, a tool that detects bioweapons must be correct 100 percent of the time. If the AI misidentifies anthrax as a harmless bacterium, the person who was infected may not receive the treatment they need.

Another logistical, hands-on approach to improving biodefenses would be to make special high-tech suits that would completely shield first responders and others from deadly germs and toxins. Although biohazard suits have been in use for several years, these outfits suffer from a major disadvantage—if a suit is punctured, microbes can enter and infect the wearer. What is needed is a suit that automatically seals itself if it is punctured. Such suits could also be put on already infected people to keep them from spreading the disease to health care workers and other citizens. This type of technology is theoretically possible: The National Aeronautics and Space Administration (NASA) is working on a spacesuit that repairs punctures with a special gel that is inside the suit. However, it is unknown whether this could one day be used for biohazard suits, and even if it could, it would be many years before the technology is perfected. According to *Popular Science*, NASA will not have the new spacesuits completed until at least 2023.

NOT QUITE GOOD ENOUGH

"Programs enacted after 9-11 helped shore up our defenses. But in their current form, they're not as well equipped to promote development of the kinds of technologies that we need to thwart modern day threats. These threats may not come from established agents of bioterror, but new strains of bugs engineered for deadly purposes."

—Scott Gottlieb, Commissioner of Food and Drugs at the U.S. Food and Drug Administration

Scott Gottlieb, "Ricin and the Risk of Bioterror: Are We Prepared?," *Forbes*, April 17, 2013. www.forbes.com/sites/scottgottlieb/2013/04/17/ricin-domestic-bioterrorism-and-the-lessons-learned-after-9-11-are-we-safer-today-than-we-were-ten-years-ago/#10a022108960.

Can Humans Be Trusted?

Some modern observers have concluded that although such technical advances are valuable as precautions, they will never be needed in any significant quantities. According to this view, any future biological attacks will be random and small scale, and they will result in few or no deaths. They believe large-scale biological attacks will be unlikely because ultimately those capable of engineering such major events will recognize that biological mass murder is morally wrong.

An often-cited example of this moral dimension of the issue is the development of biological weapons by the United States, Britain, the Soviet Union, and other nations during the 20th century. Although these countries clearly possessed the means to launch biological attacks on one another, they did not

do so. Even the Soviets, widely seen as international rule break-
ers, refrained from using their vast biological stockpiles. Some
people assume that moral restraints—certain deep-seated human
taboos and inhibitions against mass murder—were involved.

However, those who disagree with this view point out
that another nation that developed biological weapons in the
20th century—Japan—did actually use them against the
Chinese. Moreover, the stockpiling and even the use of biological weapons by countries may, over time, seem expected and
necessary rather than morally unacceptable. For instance, many
people claim that if the United States finds out other countries
are building up stockpiles of biological weapons, it would be
irresponsible not to do the same. People who hold this view see
having the same weapons as other countries as a necessary defense strategy. Critics of the moral restraint argument also point
out that even if the leaders and scientists of a country exhibit
such restraints, it is unlikely that renegade terrorist groups and
individual terrorists will do so.

An Uncertain Future

It is clear that the United States needs to be prepared in case
a biological attack takes place in the future, but it is unclear
whether that attack will ever come. It is also unclear whether an
attack will be deadly; some people may fall ill, but it is possible
for a biological attack not to result in any deaths, depending
on the agent used. Regardless, the government has a duty to
protect its citizens from the effects of an attack, including the
widespread panic that would almost certainly be a result. With
some sensible changes to government policy as well as the tech-
nological advances that are currently being made, the United
States may be able to prevent a tragedy from occurring.

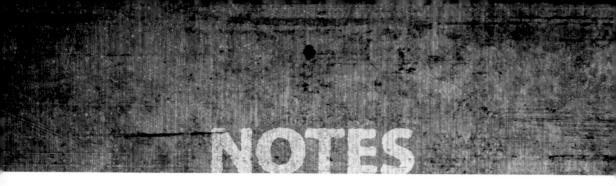

Introduction: What Are Biological Weapons?

1. Barry R. Schneider, "Biological Weapon," *Encyclopedia Britannica*, last updated September 12, 2014. www.britannica.com/technology/biological-weapon.

2. Quoted in ICMN Staff, "American History Myths Debunked: The Indians Weren't Defeated by White Settlers," Indian Country Media Network, last updated August 18, 2017. indiancountrymedianetwork.com/history/events/american-history-myths-debunked-the-indians-werent-defeated-by-white-settlers/.

Chapter 1: The Effects of Biological Agents

3. Eric Croddy, *Chemical and Biological Warfare: A Comprehensive Survey for the Concerned Citizen*. New York, NY: Copernicus, 2002, pp. 67–68.

4. Peter Apps, "Commentary: The Next Super Weapon Could Be Biological," Reuters, April 19, 2017. www.reuters.com/article/us-biological-weaons-commentary-idUSKBN17L1SZ.

5. Croddy, *Chemical and Biological Warfare*, p. 68.

6. Leonard A. Cole, *The Eleventh Plague: The Politics of Biological and Chemical Warfare*. New York, NY: W. H. Freeman, 2001, pp. 219–220.

7. Croddy, *Chemical and Biological Warfare*, p. 216.

8. Brenda J. McEleney, "Smallpox: A Primer," *The Gathering Biological Warfare Storm*, ed. Jim A. Davis and Barry R. Schneider. London, UK: Praeger, 2004, pp. 92–93.

9. Editorial Team, "What Is Herd Immunity?," *Vaccines Today*, February 7, 2015. www.vaccinestoday.eu/stories/what-is-herd-immunity/.

10. Andrew Moscrop, "Mass Hysteria Is Seen as Main Threat from Bioweapons," *British Medical Journal*, vol. 323, no. 7320, November 3, 2001, p. 1023. search.proquest.com/openview/9e885e22138430f6e9d5704bf19a972a/1?pq-origsite=gscholar&cbl=2040978.

11. "Shep Smith's Rejoinder to 'Irresponsible' Ebola Coverage," YouTube video, 4:10, posted by Brian Stelter, October 15, 2014. www.youtube.com/watch?v=Z2KBfynW09I&t=1s.

12. Simon Wessely, "Psychological Implications of Chemical and Biological Weapons," *British Medical Journal*, vol. 323, no. 7318, October 20, 2001, pp. 878–879. www.ncbi.nlm.nih.gov/pmc/articles/PMC1121425/.

13. Romeo Vitelli, "Can Social Media Spread Epidemics?," *Psychology Today*, September 23, 2013. www.psychologytoday.com/blog/media-spotlight/201309/can-social-media-spread-epidemics.

Chapter 2: Biological Warfare in the 20th Century

14. "Convention on the Prohibition of the Development, Production and Stockpiling of Bacteriological (Biological) and Toxin Weapons and on Their Destruction," Organization for the Prohibition of Biological Weapons, accessed August 31, 2017. www.opbw.org/convention/conv.html.

15. "Convention on the Prohibition of the Development, Production and Stockpiling of Bacteriological (Biological) and Toxin Weapons," Organization for the Prohibition of Biological Weapons.

16. Croddy, *Chemical and Biological Warfare*, p. 35.

17. "Chemical and Biological Weapons Status at a Glance," Arms Control Association, June 30, 2017. www.armscontrol.org/factsheets/cbwprolif.

18. Aimee Amiga and Ruth Schuster, "EU Report: ISIS Could Commit Chemical or Biological Terror Attack in West," *Haaretz*, December 13, 2015. www.haaretz.com/middle-east-news/isis/1.691157.

Chapter 3: Bioterrorism: A Growing Concern

19. Quoted in Sarah Ruiz-Grossman, "5 Things the Media Gets Wrong About White Supremacist Hate," *Huffington Post*, updated August 23, 2017. www.huffingtonpost.com/entry/media-white-supremacist-hate_us_593850d5e4b0b13f2c66667a.

20. Brian Handwerk, "What Does 'Jihad' Really Mean to Muslims?," *National Geographic News*, last updated October 24, 2003. news.nationalgeographic.com/news/2003/10/1023_031023_jihad.html.

21. Scott Shane, "F.B.I., Laying Out Evidence, Closes Anthrax Case," *New York Times*, February 19, 2010. www.nytimes.com/2010/02/20/us/20anthrax.html?mcubz=3.

22. Anne Kohnen, "Responding to the Threat of Agroterrorism: Specific Recommendations for the United States Department of Agriculture," Harvard Kennedy School, October 2000, p. 12. www.innovations.harvard.edu/sites/default/files/responding_to_the_threat_of_agroterrorism.pdf.

23. "Agroterrorism: What Is the Threat and What Can Be Done About It?," RAND Corporation, 2003. www.rand.org/pubs/research_briefs/RB7565/index1.html

Chapter 4: Fighting Biological Attacks

24. Quoted in Tara O'Toole, Mair Michael, and Thomas V. Inglesby, "Shining Light on 'Dark Winter,'" *Clinical Infectious Diseases*, April 1, 2002. academic.oup.com/cid/article/34/7/972/316999/Shining-Light-on-Dark-Winter.

25. Quoted in David Stipp, "Bioterror Is in the Air: The U.S. Has Failed Thus Far to Fully Address the Most Insidious Threat," *Fortune*, October 15, 2001. archive.fortune.com/

magazines/fortune/fortune_archive/2001/10/15/311509/
index.htm.

26. The Institute of Medicine of the National Academies, *Future of Emergency Care: Hospital-Based Emergency Care at the Breaking Point*. Washington, DC: The National Academies Press, 2007, p. 259. www.nap.edu/read/11621/chapter/9.

27. Barbara F. Bullock, "Surveillance and Detection: A Public Health Response to Bio-Terrorism," in *The Gathering Biological Warfare Storm*, ed. Jim A. Davis and Barry R. Schneider. London, UK: Praeger, 2004, pp. 34–35.

28. Steven Black, "Smallpox Sense," *Vaccination News*, December 24, 2001. www.vaccinationnews.com/DailyNews/December2001/SmallpoxSense.htm.

29. Lawrence O. Gostin, "Yes, New Laws Are Needed to Enable State and Federal Agencies to Work Together in an Emergency," *Insight on the News*, January 7, 2002.

30. "Model State Emergency Health Powers Act," American Civil Liberties Union, accessed August 29, 2017. www.aclu.org/other/model-state-emergency-health-powers-act.

31. Benjamin Franklin, "Pennsylvania Assembly: Reply to Governor, November 11, 1755," in *The Papers of Benjamin Franklin*, vol. 6, ed. Leonard W. Laboree. New Haven, CT: Yale University Press, 1963, p. 242.

Chapter 5: Preparing for the Future

32. David G. Gompert, "Sharpen the Fear," *Bulletin of the Atomic Scientists*, January/February 2000, p. 76.

33. Thomas Graham Jr., "Nuclear Targeting and the Role of Nuclear Weapons," *Defense News*, February 23–March 1, 1998.

34. Lawrence Wittmer, "Do Nuclear Weapons Really Deter Aggression?," *Huffington Post*, accessed August 29, 2017. www.huffingtonpost.com/lawrence-wittner/do-nuclear-weapons-really_b_1568277.html.

35. Quoted in Peter Apps, "Commentary: The Next Super Weapon Could Be Biological," Reuters, April 19, 2017. www.reuters.com/article/us-biological-weaons-commentary-idUSKBN17L1SZ.

36. Tom Ridge and Joseph Lieberman, "Tom Ridge and Joseph Lieberman: How Donald Trump Can Protect America from Bioterrorism," *TIME*, December 13, 2016. time.com/4598145/donald-trump-biological-terrorism/.

37. Kelsey D. Atherton, "The Newest Defense Against Biological Warfare? This Cube," *Popular Science*, April 4, 2013. www.popsci.com/technology/article/2013-04/newest-defense-against-biological-warfare-cube.

38. Rachel Becker, "AI Can Now Detect Anthrax Which Could Help the Fight Against Bioterrorism," *The Verge*, August 7, 2017. www.theverge.com/2017/8/7/16110562/anthrax-artificial-intelligence-deep-learning-neural-network-bioweapon.

DISCUSSION QUESTIONS

Chapter 1:
The Effects of Biological Agents

1. What two major factors must a would-be biological attacker consider in choosing a biological agent to use as a weapon?

2. Do you think the media should report bioterrorist attacks?

3. What could a nation or terrorist group hope to accomplish by culturing Q fever microbes and unleashing them in an enemy's homeland?

Chapter 2:
Biological Warfare in the 20th Century

1. Do you think it is moral for a country to develop a bioweapons program?

2. Describe two accidents involving dangerous biological agents produced by state-sponsored bioweapons programs.

3. What are some differences between biological and chemical weapons?

Chapter 3:
Bioterrorism: A Growing Concern

1. Why do you think the media does not often call violent Americans terrorists?

2. What are some reasons why a person or group might carry out a bioterrorist attack?

3. What are three potential advantages for individuals who choose to launch an agroterrorist assault?

Chapter 4:
Fighting Biological Attacks

1. Design an anthrax drill for your community.

2. Describe a situation involving a biological attack in which a vaccine would be useful. Describe a situation in which it would not be useful.

3. In the event of a biological emergency, do you think the government should have the power to do anything it considers necessary, or should people's civil liberties be considered?

Chapter 5:
Preparing for the Future

1. How would genetic engineering make biological agents more dangerous?

2. What changes should be made in society and government to better protect the United States from a biological attack?

3. Do you think governments that create biological weapons as a form of self-defense can be trusted not to use them to attack other countries?

Centers for Disease Control and Prevention (CDC)
1600 Clifton Rd.
Atlanta, GA 30329
(800) 232-4636
www.cdc.gov
> The CDC is a U.S. government agency that protects public health by preventing and controlling diseases and by responding to public health emergencies, including potential biological attacks by terrorists. Information about biological warfare agents can be obtained on the CDC's website.

Food and Agriculture Organization of the United Nations (FOA)
Viale delle Terme di Caracalla
00153 Rome, Italy
FAO-HQ@fao.org
www.fao.org/home/en/
> One of this organization's goals is to monitor the threat of agroterrorism around the world.

Johns Hopkins Center for Health Security
621 E. Pratt Street, Suite 210
Baltimore, MD 21202
(443) 573-3304
www.centerforhealthsecurity.org
> This organization studies incidents that could pose a threat to health security, including a biological attack.

United Nations Office for Disarmament Affairs (UNODA)
UN Plaza, Room S-3185
New York, NY 10017
UNODA-web@un.org
www.un.org/disarmament
> The UNODA oversees United Nations treaties regarding
> weapons of mass destruction, including
> biological weapons.

United Nations Office on Drugs and Crime (UNODC)
Terrorism Prevention Branch
Vienna International Centre
P.O. Box 500
1400 Vienna, Austria
unodc.tpb@unodc.org
www.unodc.org/unodc/en/terrorism/index.html
> One of the duties of UNODC is to monitor and respond to
> terrorist activity.

Books

Farndon, John. *Plague!: Epidemics and Scourges Through the Ages.* Minneapolis, MN: Hungry Tomato, 2017.

> This book discusses some of history's worst diseases, which could potentially be used as biological weapons today.

Gray, Leon. *Dirty Bombs and Shell Shock: Biology Goes to War.* Minneapolis, MN: Lerner Publications, 2018.

> Biology has been an important part of war since the beginning of time, even before people fully understood it. Over time, weapons and defenses contributed to people's current understanding of biology. This book examines how biologists and doctors have contributed to modern warfare.

Miller, Judith, Stephen Engelberg, and William Broad. *Germs: Biological Weapons and America's Secret War.* New York, NY: Simon & Schuster, 2001.

> This book discusses the developing threat of biological warfare in recent decades, including the little-publicized 1984 biological attack on an Oregon town by a local cult.

Rice, Earle, Jr. *Biosecurity: Preventing Biological Warfare.* New York, NY: Enslow Publishing, 2017.

> Studying microorganisms and toxins is necessary for countries to develop ways to defend against a biological attack, and this book discusses the military's role in biosecurity.

Vargo, Marc E. *The Weaponizing of Biology: Bioterrorism, Biocrime and Biohacking.* Jefferson, NC: McFarland & Company, Inc., 2017.

> This book examines three different uses for biological weapons and the groups or individuals that are most likely to use them.

Websites

The Biological Weapons Convention (BWC) at a Glance
www.armscontrol.org/factsheets/bwc
> This website gives basic facts about the BWC and its following review conferences. It also provides up-to-date information about which countries are known or suspected to have biological weapon stockpiles.

CDC: Anthrax
www.cdc.gov/anthrax/
> The CDC's anthrax page gives information about the disease and ways individuals can prepare themselves against the threat of encountering it in a biological attack.

Family Doctor: Mass Psychogenic Illness
familydoctor.org/condition/mass-psychogenic-illness/
> Mass psychogenic illness is one danger of a biological attack. Knowing what it is and how to deal with it, which can be found on this website, can minimize its impact.

Global Biodefense
globalbiodefense.com
> This website is devoted to news and science articles about the latest advancements in biodefense.

How Biological and Chemical Warfare Works
science.howstuffworks.com/biochem-war.htm
> Aimed at those with little knowledge in the subject, this website offers a number of links to pages with useful information written in easy-to-read language.

INDEX

A

Aboulmagd-Forster, Noha, 51
agroterrorism, 56–57, 60–61
Agroterrorism Prevention, Detection, and Response, 60
American Civil Liberties Union (ACLU), 73
American Revolution, 45
Amherst, Lord Jeffrey, 6
ANSER (Advancing National Strategies and Enabling Results), 64
anthrax, 11–12, 14–17, 22, 30, 32–35, 39–41, 43, 47–48, 53–55, 62–64, 68–69, 84–85
"Anthrax Island," 35
Arms Control Association, 43
artificial intelligence (AI), 84
al-Assad, Bashar, 43
Aum Shinrikyo, 47

B

Bacillus globigii, 33
Belgium, 51, 56
biological versus chemical weapons, 35
Biological Warfare Convention (BWC), 38–41, 43, 53, 76, 78–79
biological weapon categories, Category A, 12, 16, 18, 22
Category B, 12, 20, 23
Category C, 12, 23
Black, Steven, 71–72
botulinum toxin, 18–20, 30, 41, 47
bovine spongiform encephalopathy ("mad cow" disease), 23
Brase, Twila, 60
bubonic plague, 23, 30, 32, 51, 53
Bullock, Barbara F., 66, 68
Bush, George W., 79–80
Butler, Lee, 78

C

cancer, 23, 41
castor beans, 24, 48
Centers for Disease Control and Prevention (CDC), 12, 65
Chideya, Farai, 45
China, 22, 29, 53, 82
Citizen's Council for Health Freedom, 60
civil liberties, 60, 73, 75
Clostridium botulinum, 18
Cold War, 39–40, 53, 78, 82
Cole, Leonard A., 18
copycat phenomenon, 52–53
Coxiella burnetii, 20

Croddy, Eric, 16–17, 20, 40
Cuba, 29, 53

D
Davis, Jim A., 9
DeMier, Mark, 64
dengue fever, 53
deoxyribonucleic acid (DNA), 54, 82
Department of Homeland Security (DHS), 61, 79, 83
dioxin, 56
domestic terrorists, 46, 51–52, 54, 82
Dreyfuss, Emily, 33
Dutschke, James Everett, 49

E
Easterbrook, Gregg, 54
Ebola, 11, 21, 25–26, 47, 73–74
Encyclopedia Britannica, 6
E2 nightclub, 24
European Parliament, 44
extremist groups, 47, 51

F
Federal Bureau of Investigation (FBI), 54
Fenian Brotherhood, 45
Fortune, 66
Franklin, Benjamin, 75
French Revolution, 45

G
Gates, Bill, 82
Geneva Protocol, 36

Gostin, Lawrence O., 71–72
Gottlieb, Scott, 86
Guillemin, Jeanne, 16

H
Harris, Larry Wayne, 53
health care workers, 66–67, 85
Healthline, 21
herd immunity, 23
Hickox, Kaci, 73–74
Holland, Sadie, 49
home gene-editing kits, 82

I
Inglesby, Thomas, 62
Institute of Medicine of the National Academies, 66
Iraq, 29, 41, 43–44
Islamic State of Iraq and Syria (ISIS), 44, 49, 51
Ivins, Bruce, 54–55, 82

J
Jackson, Robert H., 75
Jacobins, 45
Jenner, Edward, 22
jihad, 50–51
Johns Hopkins Center for Civilian Biodefense Strategies, 62
Johns Hopkins School of Public Health, 69
Johns Hopkins University, 71, 84

K

Keating, Frank, 64
Koch, Robert, 14
Kohnen, Anne, 56
Korean War, 53, 82

L

bin Laden, Osama, 8, 49–50
Larsen, Randy, 64
Libya, 29, 44
Lieberman, Joseph, 83
live drills, 62
Lockwood, Jeffrey, 53

M

Manchuria, 30
mass hysteria, 24–25
mass sociogenic illness, 27
Mateen, Omar, 8
McEleney, Brenda J., 22
McVeigh, Timothy, 8
media, 25, 27, 47–48, 51
Model State Emergency
  Health Powers Act (MSEH-
  PA), 72–73
Mongolia, 30, 32
Moore, John R., 18

N

National Defense Authoriza-
  tion Act, 83
National Warning System
  (NAWAS), 60
Native Americans, 6–7
Neiwert, David, 52
Nixon, Richard, 38

North Korea, 29, 42–43, 53,
  80

O

Obama, Barack, 49
Office of Homeland Security
  and Emergency Coordina-
  tion (OHSEC), 61
Operation Dark Winter, 62
Organization for the Prohibi-
  tion of Chemical Weapons
  (OPCW), 8
O'Toole, Tara, 43, 62

P

Patriots Council, 52
Popular Science, 84, 86
Project 112, 33
Psychology Today, 27
Pulse Nightclub, 8

Q

al-Qaeda, 8, 49, 54
Q fever, 20, 23
quarantine, 71–73

R

Rajneeshees, 47
Ramgoli, James, 49
RAND Corporation, 56
Red Army Faction, 47
Reuters, 17
ricin, 20, 23–24, 48–49, 52
Ridge, Tom, 83
R.I.S.E., 52
R_0, 21
Roof, Dylann, 8

Royal College of Physicians, 25
Russell, Philip K., 69
Rutgers University, 18

S
sarin nerve gas, 18, 35
saxitoxin, 20
60 Minutes II, 71
smallpox, 6–7, 11, 21–23, 30, 35, 40–41, 43, 64, 68–72, 82
Smith, Shepard, 25–26
Sons of Liberty, 45
South Korea, 43, 84–85
Soviets, 32, 35, 39–40, 87
SpinDx, 84
Sverdlovsk, 32, 39
Symbionese Liberation Army, 52
Syria, 29, 43–44

T
Taha, Rihab Rashid, 41, 43
Taiwan, 29, 43
Trump, Donald, 83
TV Tropes, 77
typhus, 23, 30

U
United Nations, 37–38, 41
United States Department of Agriculture (USDA), 60
Unit 731, 30–31
U.S. Navy, 18, 33

V
vaccine, 20–22, 59, 64, 68–72, 84
vaccine-resistant anthrax, 40
Vigo, Indiana, 33
Vitelli, Romeo, 27

W
Wessely, Simon, 27
white supremacists, 45, 53
Wicker, Roger, 49
Wittner, Lawrence, 82
Woolsey, James, 64
World Health Organization (WHO), 22
World Trade Center, 12
World War I, 32
World War II, 30, 40, 53

Y
yellow fever, 23, 53

PICTURE CREDITS

Cover Tereshchenko Dmitry/Shutterstock.com; p. 7 Everett Historical/Shutterstock.com; p. 11 CDC/Dr. M.S. Ferguson; p. 13 LightField Studios/Shutterstock.com; pp. 14–15 Janice Haney Carr/Centers for Disease Control and Prevention; p. 19 Rd24/Shutterstock.com; p. 24 NOEL CELIS/AFP/Getty Images; p. 26 Brendan Hoffman/Getty Images; pp. 30–31 The Asahi Shimbun via Getty Images; p. 34 Peter Hermes Furian/Shutterstock.com; p. 37 Drop of Light/Shutterstock.com; p. 39 vagant/Shutterstock.com; p. 42 Barks/Shutterstock.com; p. 46 vasosh/iStock/Thinkstock; p. 48 FBI/Getty Images; p. 55 PJF Military Collection/Alamy Stock Photo; p. 57 Vladimir Mulder/Shutterstock.com; p. 61 dcwcreations/Shutterstock.com; p. 63 Gary M. Williams/Getty Images; p. 67 ChameleonsEye/Shutterstock.com; p. 70 CDC/John Noble, Jr., M.D.; p. 74 Spencer Platt/Getty Images; p. 77 Fernando Cortes/Shutterstock.com; p. 81 Michael Zysman/Shutterstock.com; p. 83 Dmitry Kalinovsky/Shutterstock.com.

Anna Collins lives in Buffalo, NY, with her dog, Fitzgerald, and her husband, Jason, whom she met on a road trip across the United States. She loves coffee and refuses to write without having a full pot ready.